THE "SPECTACLE SERIES."

A NEW AND ELEGANT SERIES OF BOOKS FOR THE YOUNG.

FOUR VOLUMES IN A HANDSOME LIBRARY.

Price, $3.40 *a set;* 85 *cts. per vol.*

Vol. IV.—MOSCOW.—Just ready.

With over thirty new and beautiful illustrations from designs coming from Russia. A charming book. Price, 80 cents.

Vol. III.—PEKIN.

Fourth Thousand.

With five full-page and twenty-five small illustrations, rare and curious, from original designs, which came from Pekin. Written by one well and directly informed of the country of which she writes.

So little that is authentic has been written of China, that a book got up in the attractive form of this will be sought after by youth everywhere. Price, 80 cents.

Vol. II.—ST. PETERSBURG.

Sixth Thousand.

With thirty original illustrations from designs from St. Petersburg.

Price, 80 cents.

Vol. I.—BOSTON AND VICINITY.

Eighth Thousand.

With over forty illustrations. Price, 80 cents.

This series of books is noticed by the press as even superior to Jacob Abbott's books for the young. *Near twenty thousand volumes have been sold.*

They are for sale by booksellers everywhere, or will be sent by mail free, on receipt of eighty cents each volume.

WALKER, WISE, & CO., Publishers,

245 WASHINGTON ST., BOSTON.

FIRST DAY AT SCHOOL.

THE

PIONEER BOY,

AND

HOW HE BECAME PRESIDENT.

BY

WILLIAM M. THAYER,

AUTHOR OF "THE BOBBIN BOY," "THE PRINTER BOY," "THE POOR BOY AND MERCHANT PRINCE," "WORKING AND WINNING," "TALES FROM GENESIS IN TWO VOLUMES," ETC.

EIGHTEENTH THOUSAND.

BOSTON:
WALKER, WISE, AND COMPANY,
245 WASHINGTON STREET.
1864.

University Press:
Welch, Bigelow, and Company,
Cambridge.

PREFACE.

THAT a boy, reared in a floorless log-cabin of the West to twenty-one years of age, should work his way, by dint of perseverance, into the legal profession, and finally become President of the United States, is a fact of sufficient importance to justify the inquiry, *how it was done.* This humble volume answers that question, by telling the story of his early life, and pointing out the elements of his success. The imagination has done no more than connect facts gathered from authentic sources.

While the chief object of the book is to show how its hero won his position, it brings out, incidentally, the manners and customs of the times and section of the country in which he was reared.

The author has intentionally avoided the provincialisms, and that singular perversion of the English language, that characterized the poor people of Kentucky and Indiana forty years ago.

Real names are generally used in the work. In some instances, however, where objections to such a use seemed to exist, fictitious names are employed.

To the persons, residing in five different States, who have promptly and cordially assisted the author, during the past year, in collecting materials for the work, he gratefully records his thanks.

W. M. T.

CONTENTS.

I.

II.

XXII.

XXIII.

XXIV.

THE PIONEER BOY.

I.

FIRST DAY AT SCHOOL.

A BRIGHT spring morning, flooding hill and valley with its golden light, an old log-house with its humble tenants at the door, and the hero of our volume starting forth to receive his first lesson at school, is the scene that opens to our view.

"A great day for you, my boy," said his mother; "it's better than silver and gold to know how to read."

"Do the best you can," added his father; "it's only a short time that you have to learn."

"I'll try," replied the lad, then just seven years old; and he went off in high spirits.

"There's not much need of telling him to do his best," said his mother, as he started off, addressing her remark to her husband; "he'll do that any-how."

"It won't do him any hurt to jog his mind a little

on the subject," responded the father, whose good opinion of his boy was not a whit below that of the mother. "He 's so set on learnin' to read, that I don't think there 's much danger of his not doin' well."

"He would make a good scholar if he had a chance," continued the mother; "but there 's nothing here for poor white folks to enjoy, so we can't expect much."

"*I* don't mean to live a great many more years, where we are known only as 'poor white trash'"; and the father said this with an emphasis that showed determination. He did not refer so much to the lack of intellectual advantages, however, as to the oppression that the poor whites experienced from the existence of slavery, though he appreciated the fact that the advantages for acquiring knowledge were far greater in the Free States.

"You mean, if God wills," suggested his wife.

"Of course; and I think it is his will that we should do better if we can."

"It would seem so; but our lot appears to be cast in this part of the country, and our experience is hardly so bad as that of our ancestors here."

"It 's bad enough; and it don't make my lot any less hard to know that my father was hardly so well off as I am. I was knocked about from pillar to post year after year, and never had a chance to learn the first letter of the alphabet."

"Your father fared worse than that. And, now I think of it, you must tell Abe all about your father's experience; it will interest him. I begun to tell him about it the other day, and his eyes were big as saucers. You know more about it than I do, and can tell it better."

"Those were dark days, and it pains me to speak of them; but I think he ought to know about it, and I will tell him the first chance I have."

"Yes, every child ought to know about his ancestors, and learn to shun their vices and imitate their virtues."

"I know that; but we were talkin' about his learnin' to read. Hazel can't do much for him, for he don't know much himself."

"He may know enough to make him a reader," said his wife.

"He might, if I could afford to send him to him long enough; but the longest time will be only a few weeks."

"Perhaps that will do. Only get him started, and he will go on learning himself, he is so eager. Won't have to beat things into his head much."

"That may be; but there's writin', too; it's about as necessary for him to learn to write as to read. I know what it is to go without either."

"Providence may open a way yet," continued his wife. "It ain't best to borrow too much trouble. We must have faith in God."

"I don't dispute that; but faith won't learn Abe to read and write."

"I'm not sure about that; it may open the way. Faith kept Daniel out of the lions' jaws, and it may keep Abe out of the jaws of ignorance."

"A pretty good idea, after all," replied her husband, somewhat amused at her manner of enforcing the subject. "It is pretty certain that faith will keep folks in good spirits, even in hard times," referring to the hopeful, cheerful view that his wife usually took of passing experience.

We will stop here to say, that this scene occurred in Hardin County, Kentucky, forty-seven years ago. The poor man and wife who conversed as above lived in a log-house, that is represented in the frontispiece, — a dwelling without a floor, furnished with four or five three-legged stools, pots, kettles, spider, Dutch-oven, and something that answered for a bed. The man's name was Thomas Lincoln, and both he and his wife were members of the Baptist Church, in good standing. Mrs. Lincoln, particularly, was a whole-hearted Christian, and the influence of her godly example and precepts was felt by each member of the family. She was a woman of marked natural abilities, but of little culture. She could read, but was not able to write. Her good judgment and sound common sense, united with her strong mental powers and deep-toned piety, made her a remarkable woman.

Mr. Lincoln was not so highly endowed by nature, yet he was superior to most of his neighbors in all the attributes of respectable manhood. He was of rather a practical turn of mind, and a somewhat close observer of men and things. He could neither read nor write, with this exception, that he could write his name so that some people could read it. His father before him was poor, and, what was worse, he was killed by the Indians when Thomas was a boy, so that the latter was sent adrift to shift for himself. Hard times and harder fortune oppressed him everywhere that he went, and he had all he could do to earn enough to keep soul and body together, without going to school a single day. He realized his deficiencies, and thought all the more of learning, because he was deprived of it himself. He was a kind, industrious, practical, pious man, and his determination and perseverance enabled him to accomplish whatever he undertook.

Mr. and Mrs. Lincoln had a son and daughter at the time to which we refer, and another son died in infancy a few years before. The daughter was the eldest child, and the living son, whose name was that staid, suggestive one of the Bible, — ABRAHAM, — was next in age, and he was born February 12th, 1809. He was not often called by his real name, either by his parents or other people, but by that rather homely abbreviation, "Abe." For some reason, this nickname has stuck to him all the way through life, in spite of learning, honor, and high official dignity. This may arise from the fact that his real name is long, homely, and difficult to utter, while the abbreviation is short and easily spoken. Also, of the two, we think the nickname is the more attractive, although the real name is suggestive of a moral beauty that challenges universal respect.

Abraham was seven years old when he was sent to school, for the first time, to one Hazel, who came to live in the neighborhood. There were no schools nor school-houses in the region, and few of the people around could read. But this Hazel could read and write; but beyond this he made a poor figure. For a small sum he taught a few children at his house, and Abraham was one of the number. His parents were so anxious that he should know how to read and write, that they managed to save enough out of their penury to send him to school a few weeks. They considered Abraham a remarkable boy, and the sequel will prove that they had reason to think so.

The frontispiece shows Abraham with a dilapidated book in his hand. It is a copy of Dilworth's Spelling-Book, that had come into the family in some way unknown to the writer. All the books the family could boast were the Bible, a catechism, and this old school-book.

He was not very well clad, but this was the best suit of clothes that he had; indeed, he had no other.

His parents did well, in their poverty, to provide him with one suit at a time. Few of their neighbors could do better.

Abraham was delighted with going to school, and he had much to say at the close of the first day.

"Much better off than I ever was," said his father. "I never went to school one day in my life."

"Why didn't you go some?"

"Because my father was killed by the Injins, and then I had to work for my bread, and besides I never lived where there was any school."

"Now tell Abe," said his mother, speaking to her husband, "about his grandfather. He was named for him, and he ought to know about him."

"Was I named for grandpa?" the boy inquired.

"Yes, you was named for him, and you ought to know what a hard time he had."

"Do tell me, father," said Abraham. "I want to hear about him. Was he killed by the Injins?"

"Yes," answered his father; "and I will tell you all about it. He was born in Rockingham County, Virginia, and removed from there to this State in the year 1780, almost forty years ago. I was a very little boy then."

"How little? small as I?" asked Abraham.

"Not so large as you are. I wa'n't more than two or three years old. I was the youngest child. Well, I was saying that your grandfather came here when it was all a wilderness, and there wa'n't any neighbors nearer than two or three miles for some years, and there were many Injins all about, and they hated white men, and —"

"What made them hate the white men?" inquired the boy, who had become intensely interested in the story.

"Because the white men first came to this country, and drove them away from their lands. As I was saying, he had to clear up land for a farm, and he did it as fast as he could, a little every year. It was very hard work, and very dangerous work, too, and he had to carry his gun with him into the woods, so as to fight the Injins if they came. The Injins were very cruel, and sometimes they attacked a family, and killed them all with the tomahawk. Once they killed a whole family within a few miles of here, and all the white men around, got together, and went after them; but they could n't find 'em.

"Well, after your grandfather had lived here about four years, and he was clearing up some land a few miles off, he was killed by the Injins. He was alone in the woods; and we thought they came upon him suddenly, before he had time to get at his gun."

"How do you know *that*, if he was alone?" asked Abraham.

"Because his gun was found where he probably

laid it down, and he was discovered right side of a tree that he was cutting, some distance from his gun."

"Why did n't the Injins carry off his gun?"

"They did n't see it, as it was a little distance from him, and they did n't think, probably, that he had one.

"As he did n't come home at night as usual, we thought that somethin' dreadful had happened, and search was made, and the next mornin' his dead body was found. The Injins had scalped him, and carried off his axe."

Mr. Lincoln continued: "You can't tell how we felt when the worst was known. And when his dead body was brought home, it seemed as if we should die. He was our protector, and the family depended on him for support. Where should we look for bread? What would become of us in the wilderness? We could n't help thinkin' of these things; and the future was dark enough."

"What did you do?" inquired Abraham, whose deepest feelings were reached by the narrative.

"We did the best we could. Your grandmother worked hard to support me, while my brothers and sisters, who were older, went away to get a livin' where they could. But two or three years after, she was so poor that I had to go away, too, and I had no home again till I married, and came to live here. There is no tellin' how much I suffered for several years, and how unhappy I was to be sent away from home when I was not twelve years old. Yet I had to go, — there was no other way to do. I must go or starve. You can imagine, my boy, how you would feel to lose your father, and then be obliged to leave your mother, and go off among strangers to earn your bread."

"God be praised that you have a better lot," exclaimed Mrs. Lincoln. "You would n't know how to endure it, my dear child, and I should n't know how to have you."

Abraham was too full to speak. The tears stood in his eye, and his chin quivered as his mother spoke.

"Yes," continued his father, "it would take me a week to tell you all I have heard your grandpa say about those dark days. The very year he came here, in 1780, the Injins attacked the settlers in great force. All the men were ordered to organize into companies, and Daniel Boone, 'the great hunter of Kentucky,' was made a lieutenant-colonel, and all the forces were put under the charge of General Clark. They started to meet the enemy, and found them near the Lower Blue Licks. Here they fought a terrible battle, and the Injins beat, and cut up our men badly. Boone's son was wounded, and his father tried to carry him away in the retreat. He plunged into the river with him on his back, but the boy died before he reached the other side. By the time Boone got over the river, he looked around and saw that the Injins were swimming after him; so he had to throw down his dead son, and run for his life. He got away, and reached Bryan's Station in safety."

"O, how thankful we ought to be that we do not live in such trying times!" exclaimed his mother, addressing her remark to Abraham, who was filled with wonder at the recital. "Now," she continued, "tell him about those children that the Injins carried off. That was dreadful."

"Do tell it father," said Abraham.

"That was some little time before," his father went on to say. "Three little girls, belonging to the fort at Boonsboro, and one of them was Boone's daughter, crossed the Kentucky River in a canoe that they were playing with. When they reached the other side, several Injins rushed out of the bushes into the river, and drew the canoe ashore, and seized the little girls to run off with them. The girls were scared almost to death, and they screamed so loud that they were heard at the fort. The men there ran out to help them, but by the time they reached the canoe, the Injins had run off with the little girls. It was now about night, so that it would be vain to follow them, and they resolved to prepare all the men they could muster at the fort, and start after them early in the morning.

"At break of day a strong party of white men started after the girls; but they did not overtake them until near the close of the day. When they had travelled about forty miles, they discovered them at a short distance. They had encamped for the night, and were cooking their supper. Fearing that the Injins would kill the girls as soon as they found that they were closely pursued, it was a part of the white men's plan to shoot them before they had a chance. Therefore, as soon as they got fair sight of the Injins, they all fired at them at once, taking good care not to hit the children. It was so sudden to the 'red-skins,' that they were scared half out of their wits, and run away, leaving the girls and all their weapons."

"How glad the little children must have been to see their fathers again!" said Mrs. Lincoln. "Don't you think they were, Abe?"

"Yes, indeed," replied the boy, with a glow of satisfaction lighting up his intelligent face. "Were they in the woods all the night before?"

"Yes," replied his father; "and they want more pleased to see their fathers than their fathers were to see them. The men might have followed the Injins, and killed them all before they had gone a mile, but they were so glad to find the girls that they did n't care for anything else."

"Nobody will blame them," added Mrs. Lincoln; "they did well to get their children again. But you have heard enough now," turning to Abraham, "and I hope you will be thankful for your home."

"So do I," continued his father; "the poorest home is better than none: I know it by sad experience."

Abraham drew a long sigh, as if relieved by the thought that his little cabin was not surrounded with such perils. He had listened with rapt attention to the thrilling stories of his grandfather's time, and he was glad the lines had fallen to him in pleasanter places.

"You see now, Abe, how much better you fare than your father did; and you see, too, why he never learned to read," said his mother.

"I 'm glad that such Injins don't live about here," he replied.

"And you should be thankful that you fare as well as you do, and make the most of your opportunities," continued his mother.

"Learn to read in a few weeks if you can, Abe," said his father; "for it ain't long that you can have Hazel to help you."

"How long do you think, father?"

"Just as long as I can pay for. I want you should know how to read and write, and not be so ignorant as I am. Perhaps you can learn something about ciphering yourself when you are older."

"Mr. Hazel says I can learn to read real quick if I try."

"I have no doubt of it," replied his father.

"And then you can read the Bible, and all the good stories in it that I have told you," were the words of his mother.

"And it will be a pleasure to you as long as you live," continued his father. "If I could live my life over again, I would learn to read somehow."

A neighbor called, and the conversation with Abraham was broken off. The next chapter will disclose what followed.

II.

THE NEIGHBOR'S CALL.

"WALL, neighbor Lincoln," said the man, "I called to tell you where you can sell your place, I reckon. You know we talked about it t' other day."

"I remember it," answered Mr. Lincoln; "and I want to sell out, and make my tracks to some place where the curse of slavery is not found."

"Where would you go?"

"I would go to Indiana. Slavery is shut out from there, and there is a chance for a poor white man to be somebody. But who wants to buy?"

"A feller by the name of Cordy, I believe. I was told about him to-day."

"Where does he live?"

"Down the river somewhere; I hain't seen him."

"And you don't know anything about him?"

"No; only he wants to buy a place about here somewhere, and I thought of you. I can find out about him, and send him word that you will sell, if you want I should."

"I wish you would; though I sha'n't leave here till fall, now I'm gettin' my plantin' in."

"A good long time he'll have, then, to make a bargain."

"Yes; and Abe will have a chance to learn somethin' this summer. He went to school to-day for the first time."

"That's more than my boys have done. If I can cover their backs and keep them from cryin' for bread, it's all I can do."

"I can't do but little more than that," said Mr. Lincoln; "but Abe takes so to books, that I want he should learn to read and write."

"Could n't he get along as well as his father without it?"

"*I* never got along very well without it: I'd give all I have now to know how to read and write?"

"Pshaw!" exclaimed the neighbor; "I would n't do any such thing. It don't give anybody victuals and clothes."

"I don't know about that. At any rate, I don't want Abe to be as ignorant as I am. If his mother could n't read, we should have a sorry time here."

"It's no worse for you than 't is for me."

"That may be: it's bad enough for all of us; and it helps keep us down with the niggers."

"You don't think so?"

"Upon my word I do. It's for the interest of slaveholders to promote ignorance, and hence there is the most ignorance where there is the most slavery. They can oppress poor ignorant white men like us more than they can those who know somethin'."

"I don't see it so."

"Well, I do; and I'm determined to go where a man is not disgraced by his labor."

"If you can find such a place," answered the neighbor.

"I can find such a place everywhere that freedom is, but nowhere that slavery is tolerated. Slaveholders don't consider us any better, nor hardly so good, as their niggers; and the niggers never think of calling us anything but 'poor white trash.'"

"I don't care for that."

"I do; and I shall get away from it as soon as possible after the summer is through."

"And your boy can read," added the man.

"Yes; and that I mean shall happen anyhow. I would rather have him read and write than to own a farm, if he can't have but one."

"Ha! ha! nonsense," retorted the neighbor. "You don't mean it."

"Whether my husband means it or not," said Mrs. Lincoln, who had listened to the conversation, "I would rather Abe would be able to read the Bible than to own a farm, if he can't have but one."

"The Bible, hey!" exclaimed the man, accompanying the remark with an oath; "why did n't you say a last year's almanac?" and he intended this last remark as a slur upon the Word of God.

"I am surprised, Mr. Selby" (this was the man's name), "at your talk," continued Mrs. Lincoln. "The Bible is the word of God, and it becomes us all to study it, and learn our duty. I want my children to make it their daily companion."

"Their daily fiddlestick!" answered Mr. Selby, contemptuously, rising from his seat to go out. "But what say you, Lincoln, shall I send that feller word about your sellin' out?"

"I would like to have you. Perhaps he can get around here in the course of the summer."

Mr. Selby left. He was an ignorant man, unable to read or write, and also a despiser of religion. Neither had he any idea of the value of knowledge, and was satisfied that his children should grow up with no more knowledge than he had himself. He was content to live in degradation, with just enough food and clothing to sustain existence. He was very intemperate, also, and so profane that he seldom conversed a minute without uttering an oath. In this respect he was the opposite of Mr. Lincoln, whose good sense and Christian principles made him desirous of being in better circumstances. While Selby never dreamed that slavery rendered his condition more degraded, Lincoln was continually revolving the thought that his family suffered from the existence of slavery, and that in a Free State his advantages would be greater.

"He is to be pitied," said Mrs. Lincoln, when the wicked man went out. "I hope you will take warning from him, Abe, on three points."

"I know what one of them is," said Abraham.

"What?"

"He swears," answered the boy.

"That is one thing. He is a very wicked man to take the name of God in vain. What Commandment did he violate?"

"The third," answered Abraham, who could repeat the Ten Commandments readily.

"Very well; and what does God say he will not do with him who takes his name in vain."

"He will not hold him guiltless that taketh his name in vain," replied Abraham.

"A very good reason for never using profane language. And now, can you tell me either of the other points on which I want his character to warn you?"

Abraham could not think of them, and so his mother continued: "Ignorance is another thing. Mr. Selby can't read, and, what is worse, he don't want to. His ignorance makes him appear altogether more degraded. You don't want to be such a man as he is, do you?"

"No, mother, I don't mean to be."

"Then do the best you can to learn to read, and

be good. But now for the other thing against which his example warns you, — it is intemperance. Mr. Selby gets drunk sometimes."

"Was he drunk to-night?" inquired Abraham.

"He wa'n't sober, though he wa'n't very drunk. But his intemperate habits have made him a miserable man."

"Does it make everybody like him?" the boy asked.

"It makes all intemperate men very degraded, and it is a great sin against God. It destroys the soul, too. The 'drunkard cannot inherit the kingdom of God'! I hope you will remember this, and always avoid intemperance."

It should be remarked, that the custom of using intoxicating drinks at that day was general. Mrs. Lincoln did not expect her boy would refuse to taste of the same, but she meant to warn him against using strong drink immoderately. Whiskey was the most common intoxicating beverage then drank, and its baneful effects were widely spread. Mr. Selby was a painful example of intemperate habits for Abraham to view. His mother was wise in pointing him to this cause of degradation in the ruined man. It had its influence upon his after life, as we shall see.

There is no doubt that the slaveholders had some occasion to treat the poor whites with neglect, if not with harsher measures, inasmuch as many of them were degraded like Selby, and for a pittance furnished whiskey to the slaves. We have just met with the following recital by an eyewitness, that illustrates this point: —

"The overseer appeared at the avenue of orange-trees, and presently drew rein beside us, his countenance exhibiting marks of dissatisfaction.

"'I've had trouble with them boys over to my place, Colonel,' he said, briefly, and looking loweringly around, as though he would be disposed to resent any listening to his report on the part of the negroes.

"'Why, what's the matter with them?' asked his employer, hastily.

"'Well, it 'pears they got some rot-gut — two gallons of it — from somewheres last night, and of course all got drunk, down to the old shanty behind the gin: they went thar so's I should n't suspicion nothin'. They played cards and quarrelled and fit; and Harry's John, he cut Timberlake bad, — cut Walkie, too, 'cross the hand, but ain't hurt him much.'

"'Harry's John! I always knew that nigger had an ugly temper! I'll sell him, by —! I won't have him on the place a week longer. Is Timberlake badly hurt?'

"'He's nigh killed, I reckon. Got a bad stick in the ribs, and a cut in the shoulder, and one in the face. Bled like a dog, he did! Reckon he may get over it. I 've done what I could for him.'

"'Where did they get the liquor from?'

"'I don't know. Most likely from old Whalley, down to the landing. He 's mean enough for anything.'

"'If I can prove it on him, I 'll run him out of the country! I 'll — I 'll — I 'll shoot him!' And the Colonel continued his imprecations, this time directing them toward the supposed vender of the whiskey.

"'These men are the curse of the country! the curse of the country!' he repeated, excitedly, — '*these mean, low, thieving, sneaking, pilfering poor whites!* They teach our negroes to steal; *they sell them liquor;* they do everything to corrupt and demoralize them. That 's how they live. The slaves are respectable, compared to them. They ought to be slaves themselves.'"

Now this incident discloses the fact, that some of the poor whites give occasion for the slaveholders to treat them with contempt, on account of their doling out liquor to negroes, and in other ways inciting them to evil deeds. Some of the oppression experienced by the poor whites may arise from this; and yet the views of Mr. Lincoln were correct in the main, namely, that the whites were oppressed on account of the disgrace that slavery attached to labor. One poor drunken white like Selby might sell liquor to the negroes, and encourage them to steal; but this would furnish no reason for treating a temperate, honest, pious man like Lincoln with contempt. It was only the presence of slavery that could do this.

No wonder that Mr. Lincoln was hostile to the system! nor that he was resolved to get away from it with his family as soon as possible! For a series of years he had been feeling more and more deeply upon the subject, until he had fully resolved to remove to a Free State.

III.

A BRIGHTER PROSPECT.

FOUR weeks passed.

"I've seen Mr. Hazel to-day," said Mr. Lincoln to his wife.

"And what does he say about Abe?" she inquired.

"That he is gettin' along the best of any boy he has had."

"I knew that he was gettin' along well, because I have tried him. He will be able to read some before long."

"So Hazel said."

"How about his conduct?"

"He don't want no better boy than he is."

"Did he say so?"

"Yes, he gave him just as good a name as he could."

"I'm glad of that, though it is no more than I expected."

"So am I glad; I want he should learn to read before we move away."

"Then you really think you shall go."

"Certainly I do, if I can sell out."

"You 've heard nothing from the man that Selby told about?"

"Not a word, though he may get around yet."

"Suppose he does not?"

"There will be somebody to buy, I have no doubt."

"I don't know about that; it is a hard place to sell anything here. Perhaps we shall have to stay awhile longer."

She was preparing his mind for disappointment, in case they did not sell. He was so determined in this regard, that a failure to dispose of his place might dishearten him.

"It will be better, then, to give the place away, and begin new in free Indiana," answered Mr. Lincoln.

"Well, time will prove all things: we must learn to labor and wait."

"We 've got that lesson pretty well learned now, I should think," replied her husband.

"And shall be none the worse for it," she answered. "But here comes Abe." And he came in, saying: "Father, there 's a man coming here."

"What man?"

"I don't know; but I saw him coming this way. There he is now"; and he pointed across the field.

"It 's Selby, ain't it?" inquired his father, without looking.

"No, it is n't Selby," answered his wife, as she looked towards him. "It 's a stranger, and he is certainly coming here." The man was now approaching the house, and Mr. Lincoln stepped to the door to meet him.

"Is this Mr. Lincoln?" inquired the stranger, presenting his hand.

"That 's my name."

"And my name is Colby," continued the man.

"O yes, Mr. Selby was speaking of you some weeks ago. Walk in." The man walked in and took a stool (we can't say chair, since the house was furnished with none).

"You wish to sell your place, I understand," said Colby.

"I 've been thinkin' of it."

"So Mr. Selby tells me, and I 've come to inquire about it."

"Then you want to buy, do you?"

"If I can get suited, I do."

"I don't want to leave my place till fall, if I sell. After my crops are gathered, I shall be ready to quit."

"I should n't object to that. I can wait till that time for a place that suits me."

"Then let us take a look about, and see how you like." And Mr. Lincoln proceeded to show the man his humble place. He took him out doors, and directed his attention to whatever of interest there was. He thought he now saw an opportunity to dispose of his place, and he was gratified with the prospect. He assured the man that he would sell on the most reasonable terms.

"It is only on such terms that I can think of buying," said Colby.

"Perhaps you want more of a place than this," replied Mr. Lincoln.

"No; I can't shoulder much of a homestead. This is about what I want. Poor men must do as they can, and not as they want to."

"I know that by my own experience," responded Mr. Lincoln. "I 've tugged away ever since I was big enough to work to get bread to eat."

"So have I; and after many years of hard labor I have not more than enough to buy such a place as this."

"And you ought to be thankful for as much as that, in a Slave State. The fact is, the poor whites have no better chance than the niggers here, and I am sick of it."

"That won't mend the matter, as I see."

"What?"

"Why, to be sick of it."

"Perhaps not; but I shall try what there is in a Free State to do it."

"That 's too venturesome for me."

"'Nothing venture, nothing win,' is the old saying; and as for me, I 've not much to lose, though I hope to gain much."

"Well, now, we are gettin' off the subject. What 's the damage for such a place?" said Colby.

"I hardly know myself. I think we might as well leave that till fall, when I get ready to sell. I have no doubt that I shall suit you on the price."

"So be it. I sha'n't press the matter."

"About the first of October, if you are here, I shall be ready to strike a bargain," added Mr. Lincoln. "I don't think we shall have any trouble about that."

"And you will not sell to any one else till I have had the offer of the place?"

"No; the first chance is yours."

"I agree to that arrangement, and your wife and this bright-eyed boy (patting Abraham on the head) are witnesses to the plan."

"We 'll try to be faithful ones, too," said Mrs. Lincoln, who felt, by this time, that her recent words about not being able to sell the place would prove false. "We shall be glad to see you at the time appointed, and trust that both parties will be satisfied."

Mr. Colby bade the family "good-by," and left, with the promise to see them again the last of September or the first of October. He was as well pleased as they, and both parties congratulated themselves upon their promised good fortune. Mr. Lincoln could see a brighter prospect.

"A good sort of a man, I reckon," said Mr. Lincoln, "though he seems well satisfied to stay in old Kentucky. Slavery don't trouble him much, I s'pose."

"It may be fortunate that we don't all think alike," said his wife, "or everybody would move out of Kentucky, and leave it deserted."

Mr. Lincoln smiled at this remark, and contented himself with *looking* what he thought.

Abraham went on with his school. Every day he posted away with the old spelling-book to Hazel's cabin, where he tried as hard to learn as any boy who ever studied his Ab's. He carried his book home at night, and puzzled his active brain over what he had learned during the day. He cared for nothing but his book now. His highest ambition was to learn to read as well as his mother could. As she gathered the family around her, and read the Bible to them each day, and particularly as she read it upon the Sabbath much of the time, he almost envied her the blessed privilege of reading. He longed for the day to come when he could read aloud from that revered volume. Beyond that privilege he did not look. To be able to read was boon enough for him, without looking for anything beyond.

It is not strange that he made progress, and satisfied both teacher and parents. Though a little boy only seven years old, and living where teachers themselves were so ignorant that seven-year-old boys of New England at this day could instruct them, yet he devoted himself to learning to read with an energy and enthusiasm that insured success.

Not far from this time, Mr. Elkins, a preacher of the Baptist denomination, who sometimes preached in the vicinity, called to see them. He was one of the genuine pioneer preachers, and a great favorite with the family. Abraham cherished for him profound respect, and loved to see his face.

"Why, Mr. Elkins, how glad I am to see you!" exclaimed Mrs. Lincoln, shaking his hand heartily.

"Yes, the Lord has brought me around once more," he answered; "and how are you and your family? I hope the Lord has been gracious to you."

"More so than we deserve. But you are going to preach here to-morrow, are you?" It was Saturday, and she inferred that he had come to preach in the vicinity, according to his custom.

"I wish I was, but I am sorry to disappoint you. I expect to be here one week from to-morrow, and I came this way to-day to give the notice. I know that if I tell you of an appointment, you will see that people are notified. But here is my little boy; how do you do, Abe?" And he drew the child to himself in his familiar and affectionate way. He had not observed him before. Abraham replied in his respectful and manly way.

"Abe goes to school now," said his mother.

"He does? That's right, and I hope you'll make a scholar, my boy."

"He is getting along finely," added his mother. "I think he will be able to read the Bible in a few weeks."

"That will be capital," said Mr. Elkins. "Then you can do some of the reading for your mother," and he addressed this remark to the child. "And when you can read, you've got something that nobody can get away from you. With the Bible, knowing how to read it, and having a heart to obey it, you will make a good pioneer boy."

"What's a pioneer boy?" asked Abraham.

Mr. Elkins was quite amused at this inquiry, and after exercising his risibles for a minute, he replied, "Well, he is a backwoods-boy, who can make the best of things in this hard country, and cut his way along in spite of all discouragements, helping his father and mother, brothers and sisters, and live in the woods, if you want to have him."

"Abe can do that," said his mother, looking lovingly at the boy, just as his father came in, surprised to see his favorite preacher.

"I was just saying to your son," continued Mr. Elkins, "that he would make a good pioneer boy."

"He 'll have to be one, whether he makes a good one or not," replied Mr. Lincoln. "I 'm thinkin' of going into the woods more than we are now."

"Ah! Is that so? How can we spare you?"

"If nothing happens, another winter will find me in Indiana. I 've been thinkin' of it a long time."

"And all because you want to be *free*," said Mr. Elkins, rather humorously. He had often conversed with Mr. Lincoln in respect to slavery, and respected his views, although he did not feel quite so strongly upon the subject as Mr. Lincoln did.

"Yes; I shall never have a better time than this. If I 'm ever goin', I'd better go now."

"Had you better go at all? Settle that question, and ask the Lord to direct you. 'It is not in man that walketh to direct his steps.' We all want wisdom from above."

"That is very true," said Mrs. Lincoln; "and I trust that we shall take no step that He will not approve."

"That is the right spirit to have," said Mr. Elkins, rising to go, and excusing himself from remaining longer. "I 've quite a journey to take yet."

"I wish you were to preach here to-morrow," continued Mrs. Lincoln. "It is such a privilege to hear the Gospel!"

"Your family scarcely need it," answered Mr. Elkins, suggestively; "*your* sermons do very well for your family on the Sabbath." He alluded here to the manner of her keeping the Sabbath.

"I don't deserve your compliment, Mr. Elkins."

"I 'll leave that to your husband and children to decide. I have no doubt they will agree with me. So good by to you." And he left.

Mr. Elkins alluded, as we have said, to her custom of instructing her family from the Bible on the Sabbath, when there was no preaching in the region. Being the only person in the family who could read, she improved the Lord's day to read much from the Scriptures. Her method in this respect was so excellent, and exerted such an influence in forming Abraham's character, that we shall devote the following chapter to it.

IV.

THE SABBATH LESSON.

IT was Sabbath morning (the day after Mr. Elkins called), and the simple breakfast had been partaken, the dishes cleared away and washed, and the room put in order for holy time. The morning devotions had been enjoyed, the mother reading the Scriptures, and the father leading in prayer. And the angels had gone up to God on shining wings, with tidings of a Sabbath well begun.

"Come, my children," said Mrs. Lincoln, "let us honor the day by reading the Word of God." And she took down the Bible from a shelf in the cabin. "Would that we could hear Mr. Elkins preach to-day! but that is impossible, and we must keep the day as best we can."

"When will Mr. Elkins preach again?" inquired Abraham.

"One week from to-day he expects to be here. To-day God must preach to us out of his Word."

"No better preaching than that," said her husband.

"And well for us if we profit by it," responded his wife.

We have said that Mr. Elkins was a preacher of the Baptist denomination, to which this pious couple belonged. He visited that region as often as he could; but there were many Sabbaths when they had no preaching. At these times Mrs. Lincoln gathered her children around her, and read and expounded the Bible. As she could read, and her husband could not, she was obliged to bear a great part of the responsibility of this form of religious instruction.

"Where shall I read?" she asked.

"Read about Moses," replied Abraham. The story of Moses, in common with others, had been read and told to him over and over, so that he was familiar with it, and was never weary of listening to it.

"A good story that is," said his father; "and you seem to like it, Abe."

"Yes, sir; but I like some others about as well."

"We'll read about Moses first," said his mother; "and I hope you'll try to be like him. He was just as good a boy as he was a man."

So she read through the whole record of Moses's life; and the children and their father listened with breathless interest, though they had done the same many times before.

"Wonderful!" exclaimed Mrs. Lincoln. "How God kept him by his power, and saved him from all harm!"

"That he might do his will, and lead his people," added her husband.

"Yes, that was it; and, though hosts of enemies and great difficulties were in his way, his purposes were executed."

"All things are possible with God," said Mr. Lincoln.

"And a blessed thing it is for this wicked world," replied his wife. "If man could have his own way, there would be an end to all peace and happiness very soon."

"Yes, the Psalmist could well say, 'The Lord reigneth, let the earth rejoice.'"

"Now read about Joseph," said Abraham. This was another of the Bible stories to which he loved to listen. Before he could talk, these thrilling sacred histories were related to him in the simple language of maternal affection, and his young heart was deeply impressed by them.

"See how obedient he was," said his mother, as she proceeded with the narrative. "No wonder that God blessed him!"

Again she would say, "How kind he was to his brothers, even when they were cruel to him!"

And again, "God will take care of one who is so faithful."

Yet, again, as the narrative drew to its close, "How good in him to treat his wicked brothers so well! He might have punished them dreadfully for their wickedness, but he forgave them and provided them with corn."

"How would you feel, Abe, to be carried away from you father and mother for so long a time?"

"How long was it?" inquired Abraham.

"O, it was many years; I don't know exactly how many."

"And what a meeting it was with his father at last!" said Mrs. Lincoln. "It brings tears to my eyes to think of it."

In this way many Bible stories were read and commented upon in their simple but devout manner, so that the Sabbaths without preaching must have been as profitable to the children as those when Parson Elkins proclaimed the truth.

Her reading was not confined to the Old Testament, nor to the narrative portions of the Bible. She understood the Gospel because she had a Christian experience that was marked. She was a firm, consistent disciple of the Lord Jesus, and was qualified thereby to expound the Scriptures. The story of the Cross, as it is recorded in the twenty-seventh chapter of Matthew, was read over and over at the fireside, accompanied with many remarks that were suited to impress the minds of her children.

"Yes, you ought to love him and serve him," she would say, "for all his love and mercy. He died for you, and he has a claim on your hearts."

Sometimes the children would interpose a question, as "Did Jesus want to die?" "What did the wicked men kill him for?" "Why did God let the wicked men kill him?" and other inquiries in childhood's artless way; to all of which the pious mother would reply as best she could. Her manner of reading the Scriptures and commenting thereon was well suited to call forth simple questions, and this she loved to see and encourage. The practice is worthy of a place in every Christian family.

The Ten Commandments were made an important matter in the Sabbath Lessons, and Abraham was drilled in repeating them. Four of them were particularly pressed upon his attention, viz.: (III.) "Thou shalt not take the name of the Lord thy God in vain; for the Lord will not hold him guiltless that taketh his name in vain." (IV.) "Remember the Sabbath day to keep it holy." (V.) "Honor thy father and thy mother, that thy days may be long upon the land which the Lord thy God giveth thee." (IX.) "Thou shalt not bear false witness against thy neighbor."

Of the Third Commandment she would say, "It is God that speaks here. Never swear, my son."

"I never do," said Abraham.

"And I hope you never will."

"How old Selby swore to father t' other day," added Abraham.

"It was dreadful," replied his father. "But the old sinner knows no better. The fear of God is not before his eyes."

"Can you think of any good it does to swear," inquired his mother.

"It can't do any good if it is wicked," answered the boy, and many an older head would have failed to answer as well.

"Exactly so; nobody can imagine any good it can do."

"What do folks want to swear for, then?" he asked.

"Sure enough; that's hard telling; they don't know themselves."

"It's just because they are wicked," added his father.

"Don't Mr. —— swear?" he asked, as if a man of his respectability and influence could n't be very wicked.

"Perhaps he does sometimes; for some respectable people are wicked. Sin is no better because it is done by respectable folks."

"No, never swear because you hear some one else do it," added his father. "You should n't be wicked because other folks are."

And then she passed to another commandment, the Fourth, for instance, and sought to impress its importance and value upon their minds.

"One day in seven is none too much to give to

the Lord who gave his life for us," she would say. "It is God's day, and you must remember it."

And so of the Fifth Commandment.

"There 's a great promise to children who obey their parents," she, remarked. "Honor thy father and thy mother."

"What is honor?" inquired Abraham.

"It means to show your parents respect, and to obey and love them," replied his mother. "That you can understand."

"Yes, I know what that means."

"And children who honor their parents do all they can for their parents' comfort and support."

"That is easy enough done," answered Abraham.

"I hope you will always think so, my child. Boys are likely to want their own way, and spend their time in idleness."

"I sha'n't," said Abraham.

"You sometimes want your own way now; but I hope you see the folly of it."

Abraham knew the last remark was correct, for he had sometimes been disobedient, although he was a remarkably good boy generally. But he could recall instances when he failed to honor his parents, and now he hung his head for shame.

Another point, derived from the Ninth Commandment, upon which she laid much stress, was *truthfulness*.

"Always speak the truth, my son."

"I do tell the truth," was Abraham's usual reply, and he could say it without fear of being disputed.

"I think you do; but it is well to think of the consequences if you don't."

"What are the consequences?"

"God's displeasure."

"And be disgraced among men," added his father. "Nobody wants to see a liar about."

"That is so," responded Mrs. Lincoln; "and nobody will believe a liar when he tells the truth. But, after all, the anger of God is worse."

"The Commandment don't say that God is angry with a liar," said Abraham.

"But the Bible says so many times, or what is just the same. 'Lying lips are abomination to the Lord; but they that deal truly are his delight.' 'The king shall rejoice in God; every one that sweareth by him shall glory; but the mouth of them that speak lies shall be stopped.' 'A false witness shall not be unpunished, and he that speaketh lies shall perish.' 'The fearful and unbelieving, and the abominable, and murderers, and whoremongers, and sorcerers, and idolaters, and *all liars*, shall have their part in the lake which burneth with fire and brimstone; which is the second death.'"

Abraham almost trembled sometimes before the array of Scripture texts that his mother would bring to enforce a subject. She was very familiar with the Bible, and its authority was always appealed to as above on the sin of lying.

"No; my children must never lie. Better be poor than be false. There is nothing worse than lying."

"Ain't swearing worse?" asked Abraham, thinking that his mother made that appear the worst sin there was.

"Both are bad enough, and God is displeased with both," answered his mother, "and that is enough for us to know."

In this way many Sabbaths of Abraham's boyhood were spent, so that he became familiar with the Bible. For a boy of his age, he was excelled by few in his acquaintance with the Scriptures. The Bible, catechism, and the old spelling-book named being the only books in the family, at this time, as we have said, and there being no papers, either religious or secular, the Bible was read much more than it would have been if other volumes had been possessed. It was the first book that Abraham ever read, — that same old family Bible, kept very choice because their poverty could not afford another. It was the only Bible that his mother ever possessed, her life-treasure, to which she was more indebted, and perhaps, also, her son Abraham, than to any other influence. It was certainly the light of her dwelling, and the most powerful educator that ever entered her family. We shall see all along through this volume, that this blessed book, as the text-book of home instruction, from which were derived those important lessons relating to the Sabbath, profanity, lying, truth, obedience, and other subjects, had much to do in forming the character of Abraham. That same Bible is still in the possession of a relative, in the State of Illinois.

Nor was prayer neglected. She was a praying woman, and taught Abraham when a little child to lisp his prayer. The Lord's Prayer was very early taught him, and it became a part of his child-life to repeat it.

"God takes care of you, my children, and sends you food and clothing. Every beast of the field is his, and the cattle upon a thousand hills; and you must not forget it."

"I pray to Dod," Abraham would say, before he could talk plain; and he did, as his pious mother taught him to lisp the Lord's Prayer.

"That is what everybody should do,—pray to God. They should ask him to watch over them and thank him for his goodness."

"Won't he watch over me without asking?" inquired Abraham.

"As to that, he requires us to ask him, and we ought to do it."

"Does everybody ask him?"

"No; many people pay no regard to him."

"What does he watch over them for, then?"

"He knows; and it is best for us to do right without asking any questions"; and this was the best way she could reply to some of his inquiries. It has been said, that "a child will ask questions that a philosopher cannot answer." Whether this be so or not, it is certain that Mrs. Lincoln was often puzzled by Abraham's questions. From a child, he possessed a discriminating mind, and was disposed to know the reason of things. Hence, he asked many questions when his mother was teaching him, and she answered them as well as she could.

This cabin of the Lincoln family was thus consecrated to God, and it was rather a remarkable one among the dwellings around. At that time, and in that region, there was found here and there a log-house in which the most devoted servants of Christ dwelt. Such was the case with the abode described. God was honored there, and the children were reared in the nurture and admonition of the Lord.

Mrs. Lincoln knew that the influences to which Abraham was exposed in that country were decidedly evil. There was much of profanity, Sabbath-breaking, and falsehood practised, and she felt the need of guarding him at these points. Hence her faithful counsels in connection with the Commandments.

A Christian mother's culture always makes its mark. Great and good men usually have good mothers. Their fathers may not be men of mark, but their mothers are women of noble powers and qualities of heart. John Randolph, whose name is familiar to every school-boy, said, "I used to be called a Frenchman, because I took the French side in politics; and though this was unjust, yet the truth is, I should have been a French atheist, if it had not been for one recollection, and that was, the memory of the time when my departed mother used to take my little hands in hers, and cause me, on my knees, to say, 'Our Father which art in heaven.'"

John Quincy Adams was another American statesman who bore similar testimony to the value of his mother's influence. "It is due to gratitude and nature," he said, "that I should acknowledge and avow that, such as I have been, whatever it was, such as I am, whatever it is, and such as I hope to be in all futurity, must be ascribed, under Providence, to the precepts and example of my mother."

The American nation paid a high tribute to the virtues of Washington's mother, and thereby acknowledged its indebtedness to her, when a monument was reared over her remains, bearing the simple inscription, "MARY, THE MOTHER OF WASHINGTON." It was honor enough to be the mother of such a man, and distinction enough to be the son of such a woman. And the nation, in this unostentatious way, recognized the fact that she exerted a mighty influence in deciding the destinies of the land, by the pious culture she bestowed upon her boy.

Thus our country has been far more indebted to mothers than many people imagine, verifying the beautiful words of Mrs. Sigourney : —

> "In her own place, the hearth beside,
> The patriot's heart to cheer,
> The young, unfolding mind to guide,
> The future sage to rear;
> Where sleeps the cradled infant fair,
> To watch with love and kneel in prayer,
> Cheer each sad soul with pity's smile,
> And frown on every latent wile
> That threats the pure, domestic shade, —
> Sister, so best our life shall aid
> The land we love."

In the present crisis of affairs, our nation may be nearly as much indebted to Abraham's mother, as it was to the mother of Washington. Bearing in mind his early culture, the reader cannot fail to see that it exerted a moulding influence upon the whole character and career of the son. And it is a fact from which the youth and young men of our land may learn a lesson of lasting good, causing them to appreciate the fidelity of maternal affection, and to profit by the counsels of piety that hallow the endearments of Home.

V.

THE SALE.

IT was about the first of October, 1816. Abraham had not been to school for some weeks; and yet he could read quite well for a boy not yet eight years old. He could read some when he left school; and he persevered so well at home that he was now able to read the Scriptures in the family. This was doing much better than many boys do at this day, even in highly favored New England; and the fact becomes a key to his character.

It was the time for Colby to pay them a visit, and negotiate for the place. They had not seen him since he made them a call; but there was something in his appearance that caused them to think he would come. They had not much doubt of it. And their expectations were realized. Scarcely a week of October had passed before he made his appearance.

"You 're good as your word," said Mr. Lincoln.

"That 's what I meant to be," replied Colby.

"We 've been expectin' you, and rather making arrangements to sell the place. Have you found any place you like better?"

"No; I have n't looked much. I 'm satisfied with this, if we can agree upon the price, and I can find out a way to pay you."

"It won't take you long to find out the price of it, for I have settled it in my own mind; and I s'pose it won't take me much longer to find out whether you will buy."

"I expect it is about so," answered Colby. "As matters appear to stand, it will not be a long job that is before us. What 's your price?"

"I will sell out for three hundred dollars."

The reader will not be startled by this amount. Think of a place worth three hundred dollars! You could hardly call it a homestead; and yet it was all that Abraham's father possessed in the wilds of Kentucky. A farm for three hundred dollars! House, land, and all for that! After years of hard toil and harder privations, this was all he had. Scarcely enough to supply a small family with furniture to commence housekeeping in Massachusetts! But that was his price, and it was all the place was worth.

"How in regard to the pay?" asked Colby.

"That 's important to me, of course. What do you propose?"

"I have n't much money, I can tell you to begin with, though I have what is good as money in the market."

"What is it?"

"You see I've been specilatin' a little since I gave you a call in the summer. I used up my grain for whiskey, and I bought some too, thinkin' that I should make a spec out of it; but I hain't sold but a trifle on 't yet. Now, if I could pay you mostly in whiskey, I would strike the bargain at once; and may be that over in Indiana you 'll find a ready market for it."

"I had n't thought of takin' pay in such an article," answered Mr. Lincoln; "and I don't know as I could ever sell it. I 'm going to strike right into the wilderness."

"That may be; but you 'll have neighbors within a few miles; and over there they hain't got the knack of manifacturin' it, I s'pose, and this would make it easier to sell it."

"It 's awkward stuff to carry on such a trip, though I expect to move on a flat-boat."

"Just the easiest thing in the world to carry this; you can carry it as well as not on a boat. You won't have half a load of other stuff. And it will bring you double there what it will here, I'm thinkin'."

"That 's all guess-work."

"But don't it stand to reason that whiskey would bring more where they can't make it, as they can here?"

"Yes, I admit that it may probably bring more there, and it ought to bring more to pay for the trouble of takin' it there. But can't you turn it into money in some way?"

"I don't see how I can; I've done the best I could about it. The fact is that folks around here have laid in for whiskey largely. I can sell it in time, I have no doubt, at a stiff price, but that won't help me just now."

"It seems so; but this is unexpected, though I'm determined to sell out at some rate. I must see my wife about it, however, and get her judgment on the matter."

Mr. Lincoln consulted his wife in regard to the article with which Colby proposed to pay for the place. She was somewhat disappointed on hearing of this turn of affairs, as she had rather anticipated that he would pay money for it, though it would have been rather unusual, then and there, for a man to pay money for the whole of a place. Traffic was carried on largely by exchanging one thing for another. But there was something about Colby's appearance, when he first came to see the place, that caused Mrs. Lincoln to expect that he would pay cash for the farm. For this reason, the idea of selling their place for whiskey struck her as altogether novel and queer at first.

"But I must sell at some rate," said her husband; "and this may be my last chance this season."

"That is true, and the matter must be looked at.

It may be that the whiskey could be sold in Indiana more readily than we expect. I scarcely know what to say. You must do as you think best."

"Well, I think it is best to sell out at some rate, and if I thought that this was my last chance to sell this fall, I should take the whiskey, and run the risk."

"As to that, I think it likely that you won't have another chance this fall. It is n't often that you can sell a place in this part of the country."

"I 'm inclined to think, then," continued Mr. Lincoln, musing, with his eyes fastened upon the earth-floor of their cabin, as if scarcely knowing what to do, "that I shall take the whiskey if I can't do any better with him."

"Just as you think best," answered his wife. "You can judge better than I can whether it will do or not."

After going to the man, and satisfying himself that he must take the whiskey, or fail to sell, Mr. Lincoln introduced the subject of the price of it, about which nothing had been said.

"How much a gallon?" he inquired. "You 'll of course sell it at a discount, seein' I take such a quantity."

"Certainly; I shall sell it to you for five cents a gallon less than the wholesale price of a barrel; and you can't ask anything better than that."

"That 's fair, I think; and now let me see, how

much will it take?" The reader must remember that Mr. Lincoln never studied arithmetic, though he could solve such a problem as this only give him time. He had been obliged to think and act for himself from boyhood, and of course, contact with men and things had given him some knowledge of figures, or, at least, the ability to perform some problems mentally.

Mr. Lincoln continued: "Seventy cents a gallon — that will be — let me see — seventy cents a gallon — that will —"

"Why, one hundred gallons would come to seventy dollars," interrupted Colby, "and four hundred would come to two hundred and eighty dollars."

"Yes, I see it — four hundred gallons, and the rest in money."

"That is it; it will make just ten barrels of forty gallons each, and twenty dollars in money."

"I see it. I will agree to that. Ten barrels, and the balance in money. And when shall we close the bargain?"

"Just as soon as you propose to leave."

"That will be about the first of November. I shall want the whiskey and money, though, a week before that, so as to be all ready to start."

"A week before that it is, then. I agree to that, and shall be here promptly at the time. Perhaps I shall bring the whiskey before that, if it comes right."

"Just as well, — as soon as you please."

So the bargain was struck, and Colby left.

Let the reader stop here to ponder this trade. A homestead sold for ten barrels of whiskey and about twenty dollars in money! Surely Abraham's father could not boast much of this world's goods! And then what an article to take in exchange for a homestead! What a prospect for his son! Many a homestead is now bartered away for whiskey, or some other intoxicating beverage, and haggard want is all that remains. But not so in this case. Mr. Lincoln did not countenance immoderate drinking. He used whiskey to some extent, in common with everybody else, but he frowned upon intemperance.

Such a transaction as the above was not thought singular at that day. Good people sold and drank whiskey. There was no temperance movement in Kentucky at that time. Indeed, it was not until about that time that the subject of temperance attracted attention in New England, and then it did not assume the form of total abstinence. The pledge required persons to abstain from immoderate drinking. It was not till fifteen years after that time that the pledge of total abstinence was adopted.

At the present day, the sale of a place for whiskey would excite surprise and amazement, and subject the character of the recipient of the whiskey to suspicion, at least. People would make remarks about it, and strongly suspect that the man loved whiskey more than real estate. But not so at that time, when the sale and use of it was regarded right and proper all over the country. It is in this light that the reader is to view the affair.

"You will have enough to do to get ready in that time," said Mrs. Lincoln, "if you are going to build a flat-boat."

"Very like; but I think I can do it. It 's no great affair to build a flat-boat that will carry my things to Indiana."

Mr. Lincoln worked at the business of a carpenter when he had an opportunity, so that he could readily turn his hand to boat-making. He had considerable tact in that way, and it was this kind of business that brought him in contact with slaveholders and wealthy men, who looked down upon him as a menial of hardly so much account as a slave.

"You must give me a helpin' hand, Abe," he continued; "you are gettin' old enough now to take right hold of work; and when we get to Indiana, we shall have a plenty of real pioneer work for you to do."

"That I shall like," answered Abraham; "and I can do somethin' now to help you get ready."

"Well, to-morrow we 'll make a beginning. We 'll go down on the Rolling Fork, and see what we can find to make a boat of. And we 've got that corn to harvest, too, and much more besides that to do, before we can go."

Mr. Lincoln lived about one mile from the Rolling Fork River, so that it was an easy thing to move on a boat. He could launch his boat on the river, and push right down into the broad Ohio.

VI.

PULLING UP STAKES.

ARRANGEMENTS were completed for moving. The flat-boat was finished, the whiskey was received, a settlement made with Mr. Colby, and the numerous little things that remain to be done before "pulling up stakes," as Mr. Lincoln called it, were attended to.

Parson Elkins had been round since the place was sold, and they had heard him preach once more; nor could they help thinking that it might be for the last time. Very serious thoughts possessed their minds as they sat willing listeners to him. They had enjoyed but few advantages in Kentucky, and they were going where they would have fewer still, at least for a time. They well understood this. They were about to become pioneers in a more important sense, and it was no trifling business to grapple with the difficulties before them. True, they were not going a great way,—only about one hundred miles. But this would take them into the wilderness, where neither schools, churches, nor many people could be found.

It was a change for them, — a great change, — and, as the time of their departure drew near, they realized it more and more.

"Some work to pull up stakes for good," said Mr. Lincoln to Colby; "more than I thought for."

"I know that by experience," answered Colby.

"Well, this is my first experience, and I don't know but I shall repent of my course."

"I hope not," said Colby. "I trust that both of us will be benefited by the move."

They were now standing upon the bank of the Rolling Fork River, and Mr. Lincoln was ready to embark.

It had been arranged, finally, that Mr. Lincoln should take all their heavy wares, like his carpenters' tools, pots, kettles, furniture, whiskey, &c., &c., and proceed to Indiana, select a place to settle, and then return for his family.

"Jump ashore, Abe," said his father; "you are spry as a cat; and I must be off." The boy was amusing himself on the boat.

"Where 's my axe?" asked Abraham.

"It 's all safe on board." His father had purchased him an axe with which he was going to set him to work in Indiana, as soon as they reached their destination. The axe is the symbol of pioneer work, so that he must have one to be a pioneer boy. To Abraham it was a great prize, and it was not strange that he thought of his axe first and last.

"Perhaps you won't think so much of it after you have been obliged to swing it awhile in the woods," continued his father. "There 's some work in it, you 'll find."

"Be careful, Abe, how you step," said his mother, "or you will be into the water before you get ashore."

"I 'll look out for that," replied the boy, as he jumped to the bank.

"How long will you be gone?" asked Colby.

"Ten or twelve days if I have good luck," replied Lincoln.

"If you upset in the river, we shall have to wait a little longer for you," added Colby, dryly.

"Yes; but I don't expect that. I 've fixed my cargo so that I expect to keep right side up, and sail along smoothly."

"I hope you will," added Mrs. Lincoln.

Having thus arranged everything, Mr. Lincoln pushed off the craft into deeper water, and was soon on his way down the river. The weather was fine, and the boat floated along pleasantly, much to the satisfaction of the adventurer.

We cannot stop to detail much that occurred on the voyage. One incident, however, deserves attention.

He had sailed down the Rolling Fork into the

Ohio River, and proceeded quite a distance on his voyage, experiencing no perils of wind or storm; and he was congratulating himself upon his success, when he met with an accident. By some mishap, the boat tilted, and the whiskey rolled from its position to the side, causing him to upset. He sprung forward to the other side in order to save his boat, but it was too late. The whiskey was heavy, and, once started from its position, there was no saving it or the boat. In a moment he was tipped into the water, with all his cargo. It was a good place for the whiskey, but not so pleasant for him. However, he clung to the boat, and made the best of it.

"Hold on there!" shouted a man who was at work with three others on the bank of the river. "Hold on, and we 'll come to your help." He was not more than three rods from the bank.

"Quick as you can," replied Mr. Lincoln.

"We 'll be there in a jiffy," bawled one of them, and all ran for a boat that was tied about twenty rods below.

One of the number leaped into it, and plying the oar with all his might, he soon reached the craft that was upset, and took Mr. Lincoln on board.

"Bad business for you," said the man.

"Not so bad as it might be," answered Mr. Lincoln. "Rather lucky I think to meet with such an accident where help is close by."

"But you 've lost your cargo, though we may save some of it if we set about it."

"Won't save much of it, I 'm thinkin'. The water is ten or fifteen feet deep there."

"Hardly that."

"Pretty near it, I 'll warrant."

By this time they had reached the bank of the river, and the men were consulting together about righting Lincoln's boat and saving his cargo. Such accidents were not uncommon on the Ohio, and those who lived along the bank had lent a helping hand to many unfortunate adventurers. This was the case with the men who came to Lincoln's rescue. They were not long in laying their plans, nor dilatory in executing them.

In a short time they secured his boat, and succeeded in putting it right side up. They proceeded also to save so much of his cargo as they could. They called other men in the neighborhood, and with such apparatus as the vicinity afforded, they raked the river, and recovered a part of his carpenters' tools, axes, a spider, and some other articles. By much perseverance and hard labor they succeeded in saving three barrels of the whiskey. All these articles were reloaded upon Lincoln's boat, and, with many thanks to the kind-hearted men for their assistance, he proceeded on his way.

Before starting again, however, he consulted the men who aided him with regard to the future of his way; and he decided, in view of the information derived from them, to land at Thompson's Ferry, and there secure a team to convey his goods into the interior. He had previously settled in his mind what part of Indiana he should make his home, — not the exact spot, but about the distance he should go from the Ohio River.

Accordingly he took his boat and goods to Thompson's Ferry, and there he found a man by the name of Posey, whom he hired to take him eighteen miles into Spencer County. This Posey owned a yoke of oxen, and was quite well acquainted with that section of country.

"No road into that county," said he. "We shall have to pick our way, and use the axe some at that."

"I 'm sorry for that," answered Lincoln. "Are there no settlers in that region?"

"Yes; here and there one, and they 'll be right glad to see you. We can put it through, if you say so."

"Put it through, then, I say," — a reply that was characteristic of Mr. Lincoln, who possessed remarkable resolution and force of character.

The man agreed to carry his goods to his place of destination, and take his boat for pay. Lincoln would have no further use for his boat, so that it was a good bargain for him, and equally good for Posey, who wanted a boat.

Accordingly the team was loaded with his effects, and they were soon on their way. But within a few miles they were obliged to use the axe to make a road.

"Just as I expected," said Posey. "I have been through the mill."

"How far do you expect we shall have to cut through places like this?" inquired Lincoln.

"Far enough, I've no doubt; this is a real wil derness."

"Then we must go at it, if we'd see the end soon."

"Yes; and hard work, too, it will be." And, without wasting time or breath on words, they proceeded to cut a road before them.

"I've cut through miles of just such a wilderness as this," said Posey; "and I shouldn't be surprised if we had to cut a road half the way."

"I hope not," answered Lincoln. "If I thought so, I should almost wish myself back in Kentucky."

"Should, ha?"

"Yes; it would be an everlasting job to cut through to where I'm goin'."

"Well, I don't suppose it will be as tough as this much of the way, but bad enough, no doubt."

So with the resolution of veteran pioneers they toiled on, sometimes being able to pick their way for a long distance without chopping, and then coming to a stand-still in consequence of dense forests. Suffice to say, that they were obliged to cut a road so much of the way that several days were employed in going eighteen miles. It was a difficult, wearisome, trying journey, and Mr. Lincoln often said, that he never passed through a harder experience than he did in going from Thompson's Ferry to Spencer County, Indiana.

Some five or six miles south of their place of destination they passed the cabin of a hospitable settler, who gave them a hearty welcome, and such refreshments as his humble abode contained. He was well acquainted with all that region, too, and suggested to Mr. Lincoln the spot upon which he decided to erect his cabin, and also volunteered to accompany them thither.

The settlers at that day delighted to see others coming to their vicinity to dwell, thus increasing their neighbors, and removing somewhat the loneliness of pioneer life. They were ever ready to lend a helping-hand to new-comers, and to share with them the scanty blessings that Providence allowed them.

Mr. Lincoln was glad to reach the end of his journey; and he found the spot suggested by his new friend in the cabin, whose name was Wood, a very inviting one.

"Better than I expected," said Lincoln. "I would n't ask for a better place than this."

"I 've had my eye on it some time," replied Wood.

"Chance for more settlers, though," continued Lincoln. "One cabin in eighteen miles ain't very thick."

"That 's so," added Posey. "There 's elbow-room for a few more families, and it won't be long before they 'll be here."

"But you 've neighbors nearer than that," said Wood. "There 's one family not more than two miles east of here."

"Then I shall have two neighbors," said Lincoln.

"And there are two other families within six or eight miles, — one of them is north, and the other west," continued Wood. "The fact is, people are flockin' into this Free State fast."

"That 's why I 've come," answered Lincoln. "I 've got enough of slavery, if I live to be as old as Methuselah."

"That 's it. I know just how you feel. I lived in Kentucky myself, till about ten years ago."

We must not dwell. Posey returned with his team to Thompson's Ferry, and Mr. Lincoln, having deposited his goods and secured Mr. Wood's promise to look after them, directed his steps on foot back to his family. We have said that it was about one hundred miles from his old home in Kentucky to his new one in Indiana. This was the distance, in a direct line. It was twenty-five miles farther, the way Mr. Lincoln came. It was a part of his plan to return on foot. A direct line, about southeast, would bring him to Hardin County, — a three days' journey.

His family gave him a cordial welcome, and Abraham was somewhat taken with the story of his father's adventure, particularly the part relating to his plunge into the Ohio River.

Hasty preparations were made to remove the family, and such things as he did not take with him on the boat. He took no bedding or apparel with him on the boat. These were left to go with the family, on horseback. Three horses were provided, all of which Mr. Lincoln owned. On these were packed the aforesaid articles, and Mrs. Lincoln and her daughter rode one, and Abraham another, while his father took charge of the third, sometimes riding and sometimes walking.

They were seven days in performing the journey, camping out nights, with no other shelter than the starry skies over them, and no other bed than blankets spread upon the ground.

It was a novel experience even to them, nor was it without its perils. Yet they had no fears. In that country, at that day, neither man nor woman allowed themselves to cower in the presence of dangers.

Females were not the timid class that they are now. They were distinguished for heroism that was truly wonderful. Inured as they were to hardships and perils, they learned to look dangers steadily in the face, and to consider great privations as incidental to pioneer life. Experiences that would now destroy the happiness of most of the sex then served to develop the courage and other intrepid virtues that qualified them for the mission God designed they should fulfil.

Many facts are found in history illustrating the heroism of Western females, in the early settlement of that part of our country. Soon after Abraham's grandfather removed to Kentucky, an Indian entered the cabin of a Mr. Daviess, armed with gun and tomahawk, for the purpose of plundering it, and capturing the family. Mrs. Daviess was alone with her children. With remarkable presence of mind, she invited the Indian to drink, at the same time setting a bottle of whiskey on the table. The Indian set down his gun to pour out a dram, and at once Mrs. Daviess seized it, and, aiming it at his head, threatened to blow his brains out if he did not surrender. The Indian dropped the bottle, sat down upon a stool, and promised to do no harm if she would not fire. In that posture she kept him until her husband arrived.

In another instance, about the same time, the house of a Mr. Merrill was attacked in the night by several Indians, and Mr. Merrill was seriously wounded as he went to the door. The savages attempted to enter the house, when Mrs. Merrill and her daughter shut the door against them, and held it. Then the Indians hewed away a part of the door, so that one of them could get in at a time. But Mrs. Merrill, though her husband lay groaning and weltering in his blood, and her children were screaming with fright, seized an axe, when the first one had got partly into the room, and dealt upon him a mortal blow. Then she drew his body in, and waited for the approach of another. The Indians, supposing that their comrade had forced an entrance, were exultant, and proceeded to follow him. Nor did they discover their mistake until she had despatched four of them in this way. Then two of them attempted to descend the chimney, whereupon she ordered her children to empty the contents of a bed upon the fire; and the fire and smoke soon brought down two Indians, half suffocated, into the room. Mr. Merrill, by a desperate exertion, rose up, and speedily finished these two with a billet of wood. At the same time his wife dealt so heavy a blow upon the only remaining Indian at the door, that he was glad to retire.

Volumes might be filled with stories that show the heroism of Western women at that day. We have cited these two examples simply to exhibit their fortitude. Mrs. Lincoln was a resolute, fearless woman, like her pioneer sisters, and hence was cool and self-possessed amidst all exposures and dangers. She was a *pious* heroine; and such nights as those they spent on their way to Indiana only served to fill her heart with thoughts of Him who watched over them by night and day.

We said they were seven days on the journey. Two miles from their destination they came to the cabin of their nearest neighbor, Mr. Neale, who treated them with great kindness, and promised to assist them on the following day in putting up a dwelling. It was a pleasant proffer of assistance, and it served to make them happier as they laid down in their blankets on the first night of their residence in Spencer County, Indiana.

We have been thus particular, in this part of the narrative, because this experience had much to do with the development of that courage, energy, decision, and perseverance for which Abraham was thereafter distinguished.

VII.

THE PIONEER BOY.

"COME, Abe," called his father, as soon as it was light enough to see in the morning; "you begin to be a pioneer boy in earnest to-day. Your axe is waitin' for you. We must get us up a cabin as soon as possible."

"The quicker the better," said Mrs. Lincoln; "if there should come a storm, we should be in a pretty plight."

"What can I do?" asked Abraham, who by this time was on his feet.

"Cut down the first tree you come to; all this land will be cleared in time, and no matter how quick the trees fall."

"But you want trees cut first for the house, don't you?"

"Yes, any of them will do for that. You can't do much; but every little helps, and you must begin, if you are goin' to be a pioneer." And Abraham went at it.

Sure enough, there he is, a boy only eight years old, cutting away at a tree, to aid his father in rearing a cabin to shelter them. Nor is he to stop when the dwelling is completed, for there are acres of land around that are to be cleared for a farm. On that eventful morning he began to swing the axe, and he continued at the business most of the time until he was past twenty years of age.

He seems but a little boy to engage in such laborious work; but the pioneer boys of eight years, at that day, were as efficient for labor as boys are now at fifteen. They were early put to labor, so that tact and muscular power were early developed. They were equally courageous too. Many thrilling stories are told of their heroism, that would do honor to experienced men. One of these historic records is, that two boys by the name of Johnson, one nine and the other twelve years of age, were taken captive by two Indians near the present site of Steubenville, Kentucky. At night, when the Indians were fast asleep, one took a rifle and the other a tomahawk, and simultaneously killed their captors, and then escaped to their homes.

"I will shoot a turkey for you, mother, to cook before I go to choppin'," Mr. Lincoln continued. The forest abounded in game, among which were wild turkeys and deer, and the settlers depended mainly upon their rifles for a supply of meat. "It will take me but a few minutes."

"Abe must learn to use the rifle next," said his mother. "He can often do us good service in this way, if he 'll make a good marksman."

THE PIONEER BOY.

"I should like that," answered Abraham, who heard the remark.

"We'll attend to that in season," said his father. "You shall try your skill all you want to one of these days." And Mr. Lincoln hurried away for his game. It was not more than five minutes before the discharge of his rifle was heard, and within five minutes more he returned with a turkey.

By this time Mrs. Lincoln had some simple food prepared for their morning meal, and just as they had finished partaking of it, Mr. Neale, the neighbor who promised to come and aid them in putting up a cabin, made his appearance.

"Good mornin', Mr. Neale? I hardly expected to see you so early," was Mr. Lincoln's greeting.

"Short days these, and when a family is without shelter, we must make the most of time," replied Mr. Neale. "But here is a piece of venison which my wife sent. She thought how good such a bite would have tasted to her two years ago, when we were doin' just what you are now."

"She is very kind," answered Mrs. Lincoln, taking the meat, and removing the cloth from it. "And it is all nicely cooked, too."

"Yes, she thought she could do that better than you can just now."

"How thoughtful she is! I hope we shall make as good neighbors to her as she is to us."

"I've just shot a turkey," said Mr. Lincoln.

"and my wife was goin' to try her hand at cookin' it. Game must be very plenty here."

"It can't be plentier; no danger of starvin' here; you can shoot deer and turkeys enough by goin' ten rods for your family the year round."

"That 's a fine thing for pioneers like us."

"We could n't do much if it wa'n't so."

"That 's certain; I should hardly dare to get so far away from people if it wa'n't so."

"Nor anybody else. But I come to work; and now just tell me where to go at it, and I 'll waste no more time. By the way, ain't this a real pleasant spot to camp down in?"

"I don't think we could have found a pleasanter one," answered Mrs. Lincoln.

Mr. Lincoln and his new friend Neale, with little Abraham, proceeded to chopping trees, and preparing the logs for the house. For a boy of his age, Abraham exhibited remarkable tact and endurance, so much so as to elicit remarks from all, together with cautions against overdoing. His interest and energy in the new work denoted that he would be a pioneer boy of mark.

"Better build your home like mine," said Neale; "it 's easy made and handy. There 's nothing better than a half-faced camp."

"I 'd as quick have that as any; I want to get our heads covered pretty soon. In fact, that was the kind of cabin we had in Kentucky."

"It won't take long to do that. We can cut nearly logs enough to-day; and then we can put it through in a hurry."

"Can you help me through with it?"

"O yes; that's what I'm goin' to do. I can do it as well as not."

"I'll try that you sha'n't be a loser. Perhaps you will want a good turn done you one of these days."

"No doubt I shall want a good many of them. There's Abe (and he glanced his eye at the boy, who was listening, evidently intending to compliment him), he'll make such a worker that I shall want to have him try his hand for me some time."

"He'll like to do it, I'm thinkin'. Abe hain't a lazy bone in him."

"He'd work 'em all out, if he had, pretty soon, I reckon." Mr. Neale intended this remark for Abraham's ear, and the lad received it in the same spirit that it was given.

Thus chatting, working, and planning, the day was spent, — the first day of Abraham's actual pioneer life, — and much was done towards rearing an abode. On the following day, Mr. Wood, who had learned of their arrival, tendered his assistance.

We have not time to enter into particulars about the house-building. We can say no more, than that the house was ready to receive its tenants in two days, although it was not then completed. It was so far along, however, as to afford convenient shelter. We will give a description of it, furnished by one who often found shelter under its roof, and who lived many years close by it.

It was sixteen by eighteen feet in size, without a floor, the logs put together at the corners by the usual method of notching them, and the cracks between them stopped with clay. It had a shed-roof, covered with slabs or clapboards split from logs. It contained but one room, except overhead slabs were laid across the logs, so as to make a chamber, to which access was had by a ladder in one corner. It had one door and one window. The latter, however, was so ingeniously constructed, that it deserves particular attention. Mr. Lincoln made a sash of the size of four six-by-eight squares of glass, and, in place of glass, which could not be obtained in that region, he took the skin that covers the fat portion of a hog, called the leaves, and drew it over the sash tight. This furnished a very good substitute for glass; and the contrivance reflected some credit upon the inventive genius of the builder.

The cabin was furnished by Mr. Lincoln and Abraham without other assistance, and we will give some account of the way of doing it.

"Bring me the auger, Abe," said his father, "and that measure, too; we must have a bedstead now."

"I can bore the holes," answered Abraham, at the same time bringing the auger and measure.

"No, you can't. It 's tough work to bore two-inch holes into such logs as these. But you can go and find me a stick for a post, and two others to lay on it."

"That all?"

"Yes, that 's all. I'll just make it in that corner, and then I shall have but two holes to bore, and one post to set up. It 's not more than an hour's work."

By making the bedstead in the corner, the work was but small. He measured off eight feet on one side, and bored one hole, then four and a half feet on the end, and bored another hole. Then setting up the post in its place, two sticks from each auger-hole would meet on the post, thus making the framework of the bed. This was soon done.

"Now for the bed-cord, Abe," said his father, jocosely. "We must have something to lay the bed on."

"I thought you laid on slabs," answered Abraham, not exactly comprehending the drift of his father's remark.

"We have n't any other bed-cord, so pass me some of those yonder." The slabs used to lay over the bed-frame were like those on the roof.

"How many shall I bring?" and he began to pass the slabs.

"About six, I think, will do it."

They were soon brought, and the bed was complete.

"Now a sackful of straw on that will make a fine bed." Dry leaves, hay and husks were sometimes used for this purpose. Few had feathers in that region.

"You must keep on with your cabinet-making," said Mrs. Lincoln. "We need a table as much as a bed."

"Of course. That comes next," replied her husband. "The legs for it are all ready."

"Where are they?" inquired Abraham.

"Out there," pointing to a small pile of limbs, sticks, and slabs. Abraham went after them, while his father sawed off a puncheon of the required length for the table. A puncheon was made by splitting a log eighteen inches, more or less, in diameter, the flat side laid uppermost. Puncheons were used in this way to make tables, stools, and floors.

By the time Abraham had brought the sticks for the legs of the table, his father had the table part all ready, and was proceeding to bore the holes for the legs.

"Now you may bring some more of those sticks in the pile, — the shortest of them I shall want next?"

"What for?"

"O, we must have some chairs now; we 've set on the ground long enough. I want the sticks for legs."

"Enough for one stool each now will do. We 'll make some extra ones when we get over our hurry. Four times three are twelve: I shall want twelve."

"Must they be just alike?"

"No; you can't find two alike, hardly. If they are too long, I can saw them the right length."

All this time the work of making the table went on. As Abraham had so large a number of stool-legs to select and bring from the pile, the table was nearly completed when his part of the work was done.

"A scrumptious table, I 'm thinkin'," said Mr. Lincoln, as he surveyed it when it was fairly on its legs. "Pioneer cabinet-work ain't handsome, but it 's durable."

"And useful, too," said his wife. "Two of them would n't come amiss."

"No; and when I get time we 'll have another. Perhaps Abe can make you one some time. Can't you make a table, Abe?"

"I can try it."

"Well, you ought to succeed, now you have seen me do it. You can try your hand at it some day. But now for the stools."

A good slab was selected, of which four stools could be made; and before night the house was furnished at small expense. A bed, table, and stools constituted the furniture of this pioneer home, in which Abraham spent twelve years of his eventful life.

Abraham occupied the loft above, ascending to his lodgings by the ladder. It was his parlor-chamber, where he slept soundly at night on the loose floor, with no other bedding than blankets. Here year after year he reposed nightly with as much content and bliss as we usually find in the mansions of the rich. He had never known better fare than this; and perhaps, at that age, he did not expect a larger share of worldly goods.

Here, reader, you have a view of the pioneer boy's early home. Do you like it? How does it compare with your own? There were not many attractions about it certainly. It does not look as if the poor boy in that floorless, dismal cabin would ever make his mark in the world. But "where there's a will, there's a way." His condition could not be much more deplorable, so far as external circumstances are concerned. But then he had Christian parents to instruct and guide him, and a high and noble purpose animated his soul. We shall see how he came out.

VIII.

THE GRIST-MILL.

THE pioneer families of that day needed the means of converting their corn into meal. Meal was a staple article of food, without which they could scarcely survive. Yet there were few grist-mills in all the region for many miles around, and these were poor things compared with the mills of the present day. They were worked by horse-power, and could grind but little faster than corn could be pounded into meal now with a mortar and pestle.

The Lincoln family must have meal. Their cabin was completed, and they had settled down to spend the first winter of pioneer life in the Free State of Indiana.

"How far to a mill?" asked Abraham.

"None nearer than the Ferry," replied his father; "and they say that's an old thing that ain't wuth much."

"I can go there to mill for you," continued the boy.

"I'm going to have a mill nearer home than that, — one of my own make."

"How?"

"You'll see when it is done. This goin' eighteen miles to mill don't pay: we must have one right here."

"And it won't take you longer to make it than it would to go to the Ferry once and back," said Mrs. Lincoln.

"It's an all-day job to go there, and a pretty long day at that." She knew what kind of a mill he referred to; for she had seen them.

"We'll have one before to-morrow night," added Mr. Lincoln, with a shrug of the shoulder.

"How will you make it?" inquired Abraham, who was deeply interested.

"You'll see when it's done; I shall need some of your help, and if you do fust rate, you may try the rifle next day." The boy had been promised before that he should learn to shoot.

"I'll like that," said the lad.

"And so shall I, if you make a marksman. You can be a great help to us by killing game to cook. When you get so that you can pop over a turkey or a deer, I sha'n't need to hunt any."

"Will you let me do it?"

"Yes, and be glad to have you. The woods are full of game, and you shall have a chance to make a good shot."

Abraham was delighted with the prospect of making a gunner, and he went to his hard bed that night with glowing thoughts of the future. The morrow's sun found him up, and ready to assist his father in making a grist-mill.

"The first thing is a log," said his father; and he proceeded to look for a tree of suitable dimensions; nor was he long in finding one.

"When I get it ready, I shall want you to make a fire on 't, Abe," he continued.

"What! burn it up?" screamed the boy, not understanding what his father meant.

"Ha! not quite so bad as that. It would n't be wuth much for a mill if 't was burnt up."

"Did n't you say make a fire on 't?"

"Yes, on the top of it; we must burn a hole in it a foot deep, to put corn in; so get your fire ready."

It was not long before the tree was prostrate, and a portion of the trunk cut off about four feet long. Setting it upon one end, Mr. Lincoln continued: "Here, Abe, that 's what I mean by making a fire on 't. You must make a fire right on the top of it, and burn a hole in it wellnigh a foot deep. I 'll help you."

The fire was soon kindled, and Abraham's curiosity was at the highest pitch. What was coming next was more than he could tell, — and no wonder!

"Now bring some water; we must keep it wet."

"And put out the fire?" said Abraham, inquiringly.

"No, no; we must keep the outside of it wet, so that the whole of it won't burn. We don't want to burn the outside, — only a hole in the centre."

Abraham saw through it now, and he hastened to get the water. The fire was kept burning while Mr. Lincoln looked up a spring-pole, to one end of which he attached a pestle.

"What is that for?" asked Abraham.

"You 'll see when I get it into working order," replied his father. "Keep the fire a-goin' till it 's burnt deep enough."

"It never 'll burn deep as you say."

"Yes it will, only keep doin'. That 's the way pioneers have to make grist-mills."

"It 'll take more than one day to burn it anyhow, at this rate."

"No it won't. It will burn faster when it gets a little deeper. We 'll have it done before night. You must have patience, and keep at it."

And they continued at the work. Mr. Lincoln prepared the spring-pole somewhat like an old-fashioned well-sweep; and it was ready for use before the hole was burned deep enough in the log. Then, with his additional help, the log was ready before night, and the coal was thoroughly cleaned out of the hole, and the pestle on the pole adapted thereto.

This was all the mill that he proposed to have.

It was the kind used by many settlers at that day. It was a mortar and pestle on a large scale, and, on the whole, was much better than to go twenty miles to a horse-mill that could grind but little faster. About two quarts of corn could be put into the hole in the log at once, and a few strokes from the pestle on the spring-pole would reduce it to meal. In this way the family could be provided with meal at short notice. The apparatus, too, corresponded very well with all the surroundings. For a Dutch oven and spider constituted the culinary furniture of the cabin. All their other articles of ironware were at the bottom of the Ohio River. The spider was used for griddle, stew-pan, gridiron, kettle, and sundry other things, in addition to its legitimate purpose; proving that man's real wants are few in number. It is very convenient to be provided with all the modern improvements in this line; but the experience of the Lincoln family shows that happiness and life can be promoted without them.

This mill served the family an excellent purpose for many years. It was so simple that it needed no repairs, and it was not dependent either on rain or sunshine for the power to go. Any of the family could go to mill here. Abraham could carry a grist on his arm or back, and play the part of miller at the same time.

"A real saving," said Mrs. Lincoln; "if we can't

do one way, God has another for us. It 's so handy to have a mill at the door. But you 'll have to go to the Ferry before long for some other things."

"I 've been thinkin' of it," answered Mr. Lincoln.

"We must have a little tea and a few things to make our humble fare relish," continued his wife; "and it 's better goin' now than it will be two or three weeks hence, when the snows come."

"I can't go for two or three days; I must get things fixed up around the cabin first, and be all ready for the winter."

"That is best; and we ought to be thankful that the snows keep off so long. We 've had a fine time to prepare our new quarters. And now we 're getting settled down, Abe," turning to him, "you must attend to your reading a little more, or you 'll forget all you 've learned."

"And we can't have that," added Mr. Lincoln, "for we 'll need your readin' more in the woods here than we did in our old home."

"I wish I could have some other book to read," said Abraham, in reply to his father's and mother's words, referring to the fact that the Bible was the only reading-book in the family.

"Why, there can be no better book in the world than the Bible," answered his mother; "and you get one thing in it that you don't in any other book."

"What 's that, mother?"

"Good lessons on every page, and this you may not get from another book, though I don't object to your reading other books, if you can get them."

"Perhaps some of the settlers in this region may have some books that I can borrow," said Mr. Lincoln. "I will remember it when I see any on 'em. Till then, Abe, the Bible will have to answer."

"And it will answer well, too," said his mother; "he can't read it too much, nor remember what he reads too long. Perhaps he 'll never have another opportunity to go to school, and he can read now pretty well, if he don't lose what he has learned."

"I can read better now than I could when I stopped goin' to school," said Abraham, as if that was sufficient proof that he would not go backwards.

"I know that," answered his mother; "now you have got started, you can go along fast, and that 's the reason I want you should read when you can."

"I don't want to read the Bible all the time; I want some other books, too."

"And I wish you had them; and perhaps the Lord will provide a way to get them." His mother was equally desirous with himself that he should read other books, but she did not want he should undervalue the Word of God. She was more anxious that he should think well of this volume than of all others. Hence her re marks concerning the Scriptures.

Abraham had improved remarkably since he left going to Mr. Hazel's school in Kentucky. He had read under his mother's eye, and with an earnest desire to learn, so that his progress was rapid, more so than his parents' counsel would seem to imply.

During the long winter evenings of that first winter in Indiana he read by the light of the fire only; for they could not afford the luxury of any other light in their cabin. This was true, very generally, of the pioneer families: they had no more than was absolutely necessary to supply their wants. They could exist without lamp-oil or candles, and so most of them did without either. They could afford the largest fire possible, since wood was so plenty that they studied to get rid of it. Hence the light of the fire was almost equal to a good chandelier. Large logs and branches of wood were piled together in the fireplace and its mammoth blaze lighted up every nook and corner of the dwelling. Hence lamps were scarcely needed.

Once more we say to the reader, that Abraham's prospects were not very bright at that time. Living in a floorless log-cabin, beyond the limits of civilization, with poverty pressing heavily upon him, and little expectation of changing his obscure condition for a better one, we can scarcely conceive of a more unpromising situation for a boy. Let the reader keep this in view.

IX.

THE LUCKY SHOT.

THE winter passed away, and the spring brought forth the flowers. Mr. Lincoln was preparing to put his first seed into the soil of Indiana.

"I've been thinking," said his wife, "that our loss, when you upset on the Ohio River was all for the best. I think I can see it."

"Glad if you can," replied Mr. Lincoln, "you 're pretty good for seein' what nobody else can"; and he uttered this sentence rather thoughtlessly, as his mind was really absorbed in another subject.

"I don't know about that; but what in the world would you have done with all the whiskey, if we had not lost any of it in the river? Never could sell it all here,—and what a job it would have been to get it here from the Ferry!"

"Well, if I did n't sell it, we should be about as well off as we are now."

"Except the cost of getting the barrels here."

"That would n't be much."

"Then there 's the danger of the evil it might do. It 's dangerous stuff any way, as the case of old Selby shows."

"I know that; but I don't fear for myself."

"Neither do I fear for you; but I was thinking of Abe. You know how it is with boys in these times, and how much misery whiskey makes in a great many families. And I can't help thinkin', that it is all for the best that most of it is in the river."

"I can't say but what it is; I hope it is. It makes mischief enough, if that's all; and if I dreamed it would make any in my family, I should wish that all of it was at the bottom of the river."

"You may as well be glad now; for we have less to fear; and perhaps the Lord thought it was best to put so much of it where it could n't injure no one."

"So be it, then; but I must go to my work. This weather is too fine to be lost in doin' nothin'. The stuff is all sold now, so that there is no fear on that score." He sold a barrel to Posey, the teamster, who hauled his goods from the Ferry, and the remainder he disposed of in the course of the winter."

Mr. Lincoln arose and went out to his work, and within ten minutes afterwards Abe came rushing into the cabin in a state of great excitement.

"Mother," he exclaimed, "there's a turkey right out here that I can shoot. See it there," and he directed her to look through a crack in the cabin where the clay had fallen off. "Let me shoot it, mother."

"Sure enough, that is a fine mark. I'll load the rifle," answered his mother, as she caught sight of the fowl, and proceeded to load the rifle.

"Be quick, mother, I'll fire right through the crack."

"I'll have it ready in a minute, — don't make a noise and frighten her away."

Abraham kept his eye upon the bird, and waited patiently for the loaded rifle. His father had instructed him somewhat in the use of the rifle, and he had fired it at different times with much accuracy. But he had not levelled it at living game before.

"There," said his mother; "it's all ready, and you must do your best now to bring down the turkey. I'll put it through the crack for you." And she rested the rifle on a log, so that the muzzle lay in the crack between the logs.

"Take good aim," she continued, "and kill the first animal that you ever have in your life."

"I'll try," was Abraham's reply, — an answer that he was quite accustomed to give. He seldom expressed himself too confidently, but "*I'll try*" was about as positive as he was disposed to be. And that is really as positive as a boy need to be. "I'll try" has accomplished wonders. It has surmounted obstacles, and overcome difficulties, of the greatest magnitude. Many boys do not accomplish much, because they do not TRY. They fail for want of energy and resolution, — just what is implied in the little word TRY. Not so with Abraham. "I'll try" was his watchword and pledge, and it served him a good purpose. As we shall see hereafter, he put in practice the poet's excellent advice, and profited thereby: —

"Here's a lesson all should heed, —
  Try, try, try again.
If at first you don't succeed,
  Try, try, try again.
Let your courage well appear;
If you only persevere,
You will conquer, never fear;
  Try, try, try again.

"Twice or thrice though you should fail,
  Try, try, try again.
If at last you would prevail,
  Try, try, try again.
When you strive, it's no disgrace
Though you fail to win the race;
Bravely, then, in such a case,
  Try, try, try again.

"Let the thing be e'er so hard,
  Try, try, try again.
Time will bring the sure reward;
  Try, try, try again.
That which other folks can do,
Why, with patience, may not you?
All that's *been* done, *you may do*,
  If you will but try again!"

"Bang!" went the rifle, and his mother hastened to the door to learn the result.

"You've killed her, Abe, sure," she exclaimed.

"Good," shouted the boy, clapping his hands,

and running for the game. "Yes, I've killed her, — she's dead as a stone," he added, as he took up the dead turkey in triumph.

"Your first shot, Abe, (meaning his first shot at game,) and a good one it was."

"It's a monster, mother; see her; it's as much as I can lift"; and he raised it up to show how large it was. It proved to be one of the largest of wild turkeys.

"What's the firin' for?" inquired his father, who heard the report of the rifle, and left his work to ascertain.

"I've killed a turkey," replied Abraham. "See here," and he exhibited his prize with marked satisfaction.

"Well done, Abe! That was a capital shot. You'll make a good one with the rifle if you keep on."

"I hardly thought that he would kill her," said his mother, "but he wanted to try, and I knew he must begin some time."

"Practice will make perfect, Abe," said his father; "it's only the best marksmen that can make a good shot every time. Perhaps you'll shoot a dozen times, and not kill another."

Abraham made no reply, but he looked as if he did not believe the last remark. The turn of his eye seemed to say, "Wait and see."

As pioneer families were so dependent upon

game, the fathers and sons became good marksmen, and even the females were often expert in the use of the rifle. We have seen that Mrs. Lincoln loaded the rifle for Abraham, — an act that would almost terrify ladies of the present day. But she, in common with her sex of that period, was accustomed to do such things, so that she was not at all nervous about the matter. She could fire if it was necessary.

Marvellous stories are told about the skill of the pioneers in the use of the rifle, and good authority substantiates their truthfulness. One writer says: "Several individuals who conceive themselves adepts in the management of the rifle, are often seen to meet for the purpose of displaying their skill; and they put up a target, in the centre of which a common-sized nail is hammered for about two thirds its length. The marksmen make choice of what they consider a proper distance, and which may be forty paces. Each man clears the interior of his tube, places a ball in the palm of his hand, and pours as much powder from his horn as will cover it. This quantity is supposed to be sufficient for any distance short of a hundred yards. A shot that comes very close to the nail is considered that of an indifferent marksman; the bending of the nail is of course somewhat better; but nothing less than hitting it right on the head is satisfactory. One out of the three shots generally hits the nail; and should the shooters amount to half a dozen, two nails are frequently needed before each can have a shot."

The same writer continues: "The snuffing of a candle with a ball I first had an opportunity of seeing near the banks of Green River, not far from a large pigeon-roost, to which I had previously made a visit. I had heard many reports of guns during the early part of a dark night, and knowing them to be those of rifles, I went forward toward the spot to ascertain the cause. On reaching the place, I was welcomed by a dozen tall, stout men, who told me they were exercising for the purpose of enabling them to shoot under night, at the reflected light from the eyes of a deer or wolf by torchlight. A fire was blazing near, the smoke of which rose curling among the thick foliage of the trees. At a distance which rendered it scarcely distinguishable, stood a burning candle, but which, in reality, was only fifty yards from the spot on which we all stood. One man was within a few yards of it to watch the effect of the shots, as well as to light the candle, should it chance to go out, or to replace it, should the shot cut it across. Each marksman shot in his turn. Some never hit either the snuff or the candle, and were congratulated with a loud laugh, while others actually snuffed the candle without putting it out, and were recompensed for their dexterity by numerous hurrahs.

One of them, who was particularly expert, was very fortunate, and snuffed the candle three times out of seven, while all the other shots either put out the candle or cut it immediately under the light."

Such was the skill of riflemen at that day. Hence it was of considerable importance that boys should learn how to fire accurately. Not as a pastime was it valued, but as a means of gaining subsistence. In addition to procuring game for the table, furs were in great demand, and there were many animals valuable on this account. It was necessary, therefore, that Abraham should learn the art.

There is no doubt that the culture he received by the use of the rifle had its influence in developing his physical energies, as he was ever distinguished for his strength and powers of endurance; and that it indirectly served to inspire his heart with courage, promptness, and decision, for which his whole life has been eminent.

Time nor space will permit me to recount the experience of Abraham the next twelvemonth. We must pass over the remainder of his first year in Indiana, to a sad part of his experience, related in the following chapter.

X.

SORROW.

"ABE! Abe!" shouted his father, about three o'clock in the morning; "you must get up and run over to Bruner's; your mother is very sick, and she must have some help right off."

At this time they had been in Indiana about a year and a half, and several new pioneer families had settled around them within a few miles.

"I'll be down right off," answered Abraham, springing from his humble bed, much startled by the announcement of his mother's illness; and he soon descended the ladder.

"Go as quick as you can, Abe, and tell Mother Bruner that we'd like to have her come over as soon as possible."

"What's the matter with her?" inquired Abraham, now very much concerned for his mother, to whom he was most ardently attached.

"I don't know; but you must go quick"; and Abraham disappeared by the time the last words were fairly out of his father's mouth.

There was no physician within forty miles, and

the pioneer families were obliged to depend upon their own skill in cases of sickness. A strong feeling of kindness and sympathy united them at such times, and the feminine neighbors tendered their best nursing abilities without money and without price. Nor were they altogether unsuccessful in their treatment of the sick. Some of them exhibited much medical skill in managing diseases, having been thrown upon their own resources for a long period, reflecting and studying for themselves. It was out of the question to have a doctor, and they were compelled in consequence to do the best thing they could for themselves.

Abraham was not long in reaching Mr. Bruner's cabin. He never ran a mile quicker than he did then. He was really alarmed for his mother.

"Mother is very sick," he shouted, as he aroused the family by his sudden appearance; "and father wants you to come over there as soon as you can," addressing himself to Mrs. Bruner.

"What's the matter with her?"

"I don't know, and father don't, only he said she was very sick."

"When was she taken?"

"To-night; she was well enough yesterday."

"Well, you run back, and tell your father that I'll be right over."

"And tell him that I'll come over too, after breakfast, to see if there's anything I can do," said Mr. Bruner.

Abraham hurried home, and Mrs. Bruner proceeded to get some herbs to take with her. She was one of those motherly nurses, who was well acquainted with the medicinal qualities of herbs, and in that respect was quite equal to almost any modern professor in a catnip college. With a respectable bundle of these indispensable articles, she started for Mr. Lincoln's, her husband saying as she went, "I 'll be over in the mornin'."

In the mean time Mrs. Lincoln continued very sick, and rather grew worse. Her symptoms were really alarming, and Abraham was much agitated with fear. It was a new experience of his backwoods life.

"Glad to see you," said Mr. Lincoln, as Mrs. Bruner entered; "my wife is very sick, and I hardly know what to do."

"I 'm sorry that she is so bad; where is your distress?" replied Mrs. Bruner, addressing her inquiry to the sick woman, who was groaning with every breath.

"Here," she answered, laying her hand upon her breast, and then adding, "All over," indicating that her whole body was suffering.

"We 'll do the best we can for you," said kind Mrs. Bruner; "and I have brought over some herbs that I 'll have steeping at once. We shall want a good fire, Mr. Lincoln."

"Anything that 's necessary," he replied. "Let 's

be in a hurry, too"; and he hastened to renew the fire, while Abraham sat upon a stool near the foot of the bed, looking the very picture of despair. He was glad to see Mrs. Bruner there to render timely assistance; but the evident alarm of his father, and the apparent anxiety of the good neighbor who had responded so promptly to the call, served to make him ask in silence, "Will she die?" The thought of losing his best earthly friend was appalling to him. His young heart shuddered at the prospect.

The application of various remedies had the desired effect, and the patient was partially relieved in the course of three or four hours. Still she was very sick, and Mrs. Bruner was well aware of the fact. The partial relief of her pain, however, caused Abraham's face to light up with joy, and he rose from his seat and drew nearer to his mother, who looked up and said: "Come here, Abe."

He drew close to her side, rejoicing in her relief, when she took his hand, and continued: "I'm very sick; and if God shall call me to him, remember all my lessons."

A shadow chased the light of joy from his beaming face. Could it be that she was expecting to die? Her words excited his fears again.

"God's will be done," she added, after an interval. "I am ready."

Abraham burst into tears at this, and Mrs. Bruner replied: "We know that. If *you* ain't ready, then I don't know who is."

"It's a great thing to be ready," continued Mrs. Lincoln.

"Surely it is a great thing; but I hope your time ain't come yet."

"It's come, unless I get relief soon."

Abraham listened to this conversation, and his heart was grieved wellnigh to bursting. There could be no mistake now that his mother was seriously ill. The fact could not be disguised.

"I would n't feel so, Abe," said Mrs. Bruner; "I hope your mother will get well."

"Yes, my dear boy, God knows what is best, and he can take better care of you than I can, if I should live."

Abraham scarcely believed the last remark; for he could not see how he could live without his mother. Still he made no reply, as the deep sorrow of his heart could not find words for utterance. He was entering a new school now, and taking his first lesson.

"I think you must go over to Mrs. Granger's, Abe, and tell her how sick your mother is. Perhaps they can come over and do somethin' for her."

"Shall I go now?"

"Yes; I would go right away. It may be that we shall want some on 'em soon."

"Do you think mother will die?" the boy inquired, anxiously. They had passed outside the cabin now.

"She 's very sick," replied his father, "but I hope for the best. She 's more comfortable now, if it only lasts."

Abraham's chin quivered again with emotion, and he started off upon the run for Mr. Granger's. Just then Mr. Bruner came to see if there was anything that he could do for the family in their time of trial. His warm heart prompted him to deeds of kindness, and he was truly a friend in adversity.

Mrs. Lincoln continued very sick, though at the end of a week she was thought to have improved a little. By this time tidings of her sickness had reached all her neighbors within ten or twelve miles, and they had manifested great interest in her recovery, and tendered their best efforts to give her relief. But after the expiration of a week, she grew worse, and the slight hope that was entertained of her restoration almost died away.

"My days are numbered," said Mrs. Lincoln, in a feeble voice. "I feel that I 'm sinking."

"I 'm afraid you are," replied her husband. "You can't go through much more."

"I know that God is calling me, and my house is set in order. You must look above for strength."

"The only place to look," answered her husband, with much emotion.

"O yes! and when I am gone, you 'll have reason to look there more than ever, for the children's sake. May the Lord keep them!"

Just then Abraham came in, and his mother continued: "You must not forget my counsels, Abe if God shall take me to himself. Don't neglect the Bible, and serve and love God with all your heart."

Abraham replied only by tears and sobs. He expected soon to be motherless.

"You must make the most of your time and talents," she added, "and be prepared to follow me. And you must be willing that I should die, if God calls me."

"I can't be willing," said Abraham; and another burst of grief shook his frame.

"If it's God's will, you can. It's hard for me to leave you; but I am reconciled to it: I know no will but his"; and she spoke in a feeble tone, as if strength was fast failing her; and then a brief, earnest prayer she lifted to Heaven for her dear boy, as he stood by her, overwhelmed with sorrow.

Exhausted by these efforts, she sank into a deep sleep for a short time, from which it would not have been strange if she had never wakened. But the end was not yet.

It was two or three weeks from this time before she expired. Some days she would revive so as to awaken a glimmer of hope in the hearts of loving friends, and then she would fail again. And thus she lingered until three days before she passed away, when a change came over her, and she gradually sank in death. Her end was peace.

Her dying counsels to Abraham, like those cited, were often reiterated in his ear, showing that her intense anxiety for her boy continued to the latest moment. And these interviews served to deepen the impression of all the maternal lessons to which he had ever listened. There is no doubt that this great affliction garnered the choicest instructions of his pious mother in his soul, and made them more powerful for good thereafter.

"I 've no mother now," said Abraham to a neighbor, giving way to his grief in repeated sobs.

"And I am sorry for you," said the neighbor; "no boy ever had a better mother to lose."

"I know that," he replied; "and that makes it so hard to — " Here he broke down completely, and could not finish the sentence.

"But you 'll find friends all about you," added the man, by way of convincing him that he would not be alone.

"Not like her," was the boy's quick reply, in a tone so mournful that it sent a chill to the neighbor's heart.

"No, not like her, 't is true," repeated the neighbor, stroking Abraham's fine head affectionately; "but then — " Here he was too much affected by the boy's unfeigned grief to be able to proceed. His utterance was choked. He knew that the lad had experienced an irreparable loss, and he felt for him deeply.

Preparations were made for the funeral, such as the circumstances would allow. With no minister, no sexton, no tolling bell, no bier, no graveyard, it is not necessary to make much preparation for a burial. A neighbor dug a grave on a piece of ground selected by Mr. Lincoln. It was situated on an eminence in the woods, about one fourth of a mile from the cabin; and it was really a pleasant spot for the repose of the dead. The death of Mrs. Lincoln was the first one that had occurred among the families of that settlement, and of course no other body had been laid in that consecrated ground. The day that God caused a spot to be selected for the dead was an era in the history of that group of households.

The neighbor who dug the grave constructed a rough box to answer for a coffin. The day and hour for the funeral was appointed, and the neighbors within ten or twelve miles were notified of the same. One pious friend was invited to read the Scriptures, and another to make a prayer. And so, when the solemn hour of burial arrived, the pioneer families assembled at the cabin, to pay their last sad tribute of respect to all that was left of one they loved. It was a solemn hour. A funeral in such circumstances, upon the outskirts of civilization, is always doubly solemn. The poverty and hardships of pioneer life alone are sufficient to invest it with the most melancholy interest. But in this case there was added the excellence of the deceased, who had endeared herself to every acquaintance, and the crushing sorrow of the family. Most of all, each one felt for the wellnigh heart-broken Abraham, who loved his mother with a love that knows no bound.

The reader can scarcely imagine the sense of desolation that pervaded Abraham's heart, as he returned motherless to his cabin home. It is dreary enough to abide in a wilderness where privations come without stint, but when the dearest object of affection is removed by death, and that humble home is robbed of its charm, no words can portray the desolation that reigns.

"Not often that such a woman is laid in the ground," said Bruner.

"Not often," was the reply of his good wife; "and I pity that boy so that I know not what to do."

"He certainly deserves our pity: such boys are not often found."

"No; and with such a mother to teach him, there is no tellin' what he might make."

"Well, his mother has given him good lessons enough, if he remembers them, to make a good man of him."

"But boys soon forget the best lessons, you know; though Abe is more thoughtful than most boys are, I think. He's allers willin' to leave his plays to serve his father, though I don't s'pose he 's perfect."

"Of course not; his mother had to correct him sometimes, and whip him too, so she told me; but he 's an uncommon boy, he takes to books so; I never saw his like. There 's nobody in Spencer County that can read better than he can now, young as he is."

"Poor boy! I 'm sorry for him. He don't know what a loss he's met with."

"I don't know about that," answered Mrs. Bruner. "A boy that takes on as he does knows the wuth of a mother," and a sad, pitiful expression sat on her countenance as she spoke. Her mother's heart was touched by the thought of the little fellow's affliction.

"Would that it might have been different," added Mr. Bruner, sorrowfully. He was a sympathetic man, and his whole heart was moved by the grief of this stricken family.

Nor was this feeling confined to the Bruner family. All the families within fifteen or twenty miles around took a similar view of the bereavement. The death cast a gloom upon the entire population of that region.

That little mound upon the eminence in the woods was a perpetual admonisher to Abraham. It was a sacred, solemn spot to him. Often as he passed it, or went thither on purpose to gaze upon it, — the place where reposed the dust of his sainted mother, —his heart yielded itself to sorrow. The absence of his maternal guide created a void in his soul, and the sight of this lone, solitary grave was well suited to perpetuate the sad experience. There is no doubt that it exerted a salutary influence upon his heart, and served to deepen that serious view of life and its duties which characterized his manhood. It filled many hours of his child-years with grief, but then there is a discipline in this even for the spirit of a boy. That mute, lonely grave in the woods was one of his most faithful teachers.

XI.

GOING UP HIGHER.

IT was a great change that death wrought in the Lincoln family, and no one felt it more than Abraham. For some weeks his mind was absorbed in his loss. Not even his accustomed habits of study could avail to divert his thoughts from his great sorrow. His father took notice of it, and longed to afford him relief. At length he met with a copy of the "Pilgrim's Progress," at the house of an acquaintance, nearly twenty miles distant; and thinking that it would be a rich treat to Abraham, and serve to cheer his lonely hours, he obtained the loan of the book. Carefully wrapping the volume, he conveyed it home.

"Look here, Abe, I've found somethin' for you"; and he removed the covering, and exhibited the book.

"Found it!" exclaimed Abraham, supposing that his father meant that he picked up the book in the woods or fields.

"No, no; you don't understand me. I meant that I come across it at Pierson's house, and I borrowed it for you."

"Pilgrim's Progress," said Abraham, taking the book and reading the title; "that will be good, I should think." He knew nothing about the book. Hitherto his studies had been confined to Dilworth's Spelling-Book, the Catechism, and the Bible. Large portions of these volumes he had committed to memory by frequent reading.

"I shall want to hear it," said his father. I heard about that book many years ago, but I never heard it read."

"What is it about?" asked Abraham.

"You 'll find that out by readin' it," answered his father.

"And I won't be long about it neither," continued Abraham. "I know I shall like it."

"I know you will, too."

"I don't see how you know, if you never heard it read."

"On account of what I 've heard about it."

And it turned out to be so. Abraham sat down to read this volume very much as some other boys would sit down to a good dinner. He found it better even than he expected. It was the first volume that he was provided with after the spelling-book, Catechism, and Bible, and a better one could not have been found. He read it through once, and was half-way through it a second time, when he received a present of another volume, in which he became deeply interested. It was Æsop's Fables, presented to him by Mrs. Bruner, partly on account of his love of books, and partly because she thought it would serve to occupy his mind and lighten his sorrow.

"You fare pretty well for a pioneer boy, Abe," said his father, "as to books. I wish you could learn to write."

"Time enough for that," answered the boy. "I want to finish these books first." He was so absorbed in the volumes that he cared little or nothing for anything else for the time being. "I shall never be tired of reading these."

"I hope you won't, nor forget their good lessons. You ought to be very thankful to Mother Bruner."

"I am, and I mean to do something to pay her for it, if I can."

"What can you do?"

"I don't know, but I guess there 'll be something I can do for her." And the more he read Æsop's Fables, the more determined he was to show his gratitude to her, by some act of friendly feeling. He read them over and over until he could repeat almost the entire contents of the volume. He was interested in the moral lesson that each fable taught, and derived therefrom many valuable hints that he carried with him through life. On the whole, he spent more time over Æsop's Fables than he did over Pilgrim's Progress, although he was really charmed by the latter. But there was a practical turn to the Fables that interested him, and he could easily recollect the stories. Perhaps this early familiarity with this book laid the foundation for that facility at apt story-telling that has distinguished him from his youth. It is easy to see how such a volume might beget and foster a taste in this direction. Single volumes have moulded the reader's character and decided his destiny more than once, and that, too, when far less absorbing interest is manifested in the book. It is probable, then, that Æsop's Fables exerted a decided influence upon Abraham's character and life. The fact that he read the volume so much as to commit the larger part of it to memory adds force to this opinion.

It was while Abraham was engaged with these two books that Dennis Hanks, who lived in the vicinity, — a young man nearly twenty years of age, — called to see them.

"What books have you there, Abe?" he inquired.

Abraham informed him, and added something by way of expressing his interest in them.

"You like most any book," said Hanks, "according to what I hear and see."

"I like good ones like these," said Abraham.

"I have been tellin' him that I want he should learn to write," interrupted his father. "I can't write myself, and I feel the need of it very often."

"I should think you would," added Hanks. "I hardly know what I should do if I could n't write."

"Then you can write?" said Mr. Lincoln, inquiringly.

"So as to read it myself; I can't write very well, though."

"Well, then, what's the reason you can't learn Abe to write?"

"I can, if he wants to do it."

"I want to do it," answered Abraham, without waiting for his father to respond.

"And he can get along with it himself, if he knows how to make the letters," said his father. "That's the way he's done with readin'."

"Well, Abe, when will you begin?" inquired Hanks.

"Right off, — to-day, if you are ready," he replied.

"I can't attend to it to-day; but I'll undertake it next week, if you say so."

"That'll do," answered Mr. Lincoln; "and I shall expect that he'll make a writer with such a master"; and the last words were uttered in a strain of merriment.

"Of course he will," retorted Hanks. "If he does as well as he does in other things, he'll soon learn all I know about writing."

"And what a good thing it will be to me!" said Mr. Lincoln. "I want to write a letter now, and should if I knew how to do it. But Abe can write for me when he learns how, and that will do as well, won't it, Abe?"

"I shall like it," he replied, "whether it will do as well or not."

"Better wait, and see whether you can learn anything of me, before you reckon on writing letters," said Hanks, who doubted whether much would result from the attempt.

"Time will show," added Mr. Lincoln; and it did.

The time for Abraham to begin to take lessons in penmanship arrived, and he commenced with the most enthusiastic ardor. He could read well, and now he wanted to write as well. Nor had he any doubt that he was going to accomplish the object in view. He was confident that, if he could learn to form letters, he could make progress in the art.

Hanks was nearly as much interested in the matter as Abraham himself. He looked upon the boy almost as a prodigy, and he was curious to see whether he would do as well at writing as he did with everything else that he undertook. He was glad to have a hand in advancing one who exhibited so great desire and taste for knowledge. He wanted to see what he would make. He expected that he would make an uncommon man, and he was rejoiced to add his mite towards accomplishing that object. It was true that Hanks was a poor writer; but he knew how to form letters, and that much information he could impart to another.

The lessons commenced. Abraham was awkward

enough in the use of the pen at first; but he soon overcame this difficulty, and exhibited unusual judgment for a boy in the formation of letters. When he had learned how to form a letter, he practised upon it in various ways. With a bit of chalk he would cut them on pieces of slabs and on the trunks of trees, and more than once the tops of the stools in the cabin and the puncheon-table served him in lieu of a writing-book. His father was too poor to provide him with all the paper necessary for his scribbling, and so he resorted to these various expedients. The end of a charred stick was used as a pencil sometimes to accomplish his object, and it enabled him to cut letters with considerable facility. He was bent upon mastering the art of writing, and no difficulties could discourage him. He was determined to succeed; and boys of so much resolution do succeed generally in their undertakings.

With his two new books, and learning to write, his thoughts were too much absorbed in the matter of improvement to pursue his accustomed manual labors with interest. His father observed with what devotion he was attending to his studies, and he favored him somewhat. He was happy to witness his rapid improvement. And yet he thought the boy was carrying the matter too far, and so he called him to an account.

"Come, Abe, you must n't neglect your work.

If we ain't pretty busy pulling blades, we shall get all behindhand this fall."

"Let me finish this first," answered the boy; "I don't want to go now."

"I see you don't, and I am feared you 're gettin' lazy. All study and no work is 'most as bad as all work and no study."

"In a minute I 'll go." How many boys have said the same over and over! Abraham was not accustomed to say this; it was something new in his case. He was usually prompt to obey, even to leaving his plays. But his absorbing interest in his books and writing caused him to hesitate now.

"It must be a short minute," answered his father, rather pettishly. "We have more to do every day now than we ought to do in two."

"I 'll work hard enough to make it up when I get at it," said Abraham, still delaying.

"I don't know about that," responded Mr. Lincoln; "I 'm feared your thoughts will be somewhere else; so put down the book, and come on."

"Yes, in a minute."

"Now, *now*, I say!" exclaimed his father, in a tone of authority that was not as mild as it might have been.

Abraham closed the book reluctantly, and obeyed because he must. It was not in a very pleasant way that he proceeded to the field; and yet he went to work with a will.

"Good boys always obey their parents," said his father. "Don't have to drive them to it as you do cattle."

"I only wanted to read a minute more," answered Abraham, as if to palliate his offence.

"And *I* only wanted you should n't; and I know what is best for you. I want you should read and write; but you must work when work drives."

It was not often that he exhibited so much disobedience as he did in this case. But the temptation to read was too strong for him.

"I did n't mean to disobey," said Abraham.

"Well, I don't s'pose you did," answered his father, in a relenting tone, as if he thought that he had been too severe in his censure. "When the fall work is over, you 'll have a plenty of time to read and write; but now you must use only your spare hours."

So Abraham was more careful for a time in respect to this matter. Hanks continued to come to instruct him in penmanship, though by this time he could write almost as well as his teacher.

"You get along bravely," said Hanks; "ten times as fast as I did."

"He don't think of much else," replied Mr. Lincoln.

"That 's the reason he gets along so well, I reckon," continued Hanks.

"It may be so. But what 's he goin' to do in the winter, when he has more time, and his books are read, and he knows how to write? He 'll find nothin' to do then."

"I 'll risk him; he 'll find enough to do, I 'll warrant," said Hanks, in reply. "By the way, that new settler over towards the mills has got a Life of Washington."

"What, Joslin, do you mean?"

"Yes; I was there the other day, and saw it."

"I 'd like to have Abe read it. Do you s'pose he 'd lend it?"

"He offered to lend it to *me*."

"There, Abe," continued his father, "when we get through the fall work, I 'll borrow that book for you if I can, and you can afford to work pretty hard for a spell if you can have that."

"So I can," was Abraham's reply. "I want to read the life of Washington." His grandfather lived when Washington was leading the American army to victory, and Abraham had heard many stories told by his father of those perilous times, and Washington was always the hero of the day. It was not surprising, then, that he had a strong desire to read the book.

"If you see Joslin before I do," continued Mr. Lincoln, addressing Hanks, "s'pose you speak to him about the book."

"I will. I shall see him next week or week after."

Thus the matter was arranged about the book, and Hanks went home.

It was not far from this time that a neighbor came into the field where Abraham and his father were harvesting the corn; and his eye was attracted by some writing on the ground.

"What 's that?" he inquired.

Abraham smiled, and let his father answer.

"What 's what?"

"Why, this writing, — it looks as if somebody had been writing on the ground."

"Abe's work, I s'pose. He 's been learnin' to write."

"Abe didn't do that!" answered the neighbor.

"I did do it with a stick," said Abe.

"What is it?" The man could n't read.

"It 's my name."

"Your name, hey? Likely story."

"Well, 't is, whether you believe it or not"; and he proceeded to spell it out, — "A-B-R-A-H-A-M L-I-N-C-O-L-N."

"Sure enough, it is; and you certainly did it, Abe?"

"Yes, sir; and I will do it again, if you want to see me"; and, without waiting for an answer, he caught up a stick, and wrote his name again in the dirt.

"There 't is," said Abraham.

"I see it, and it 's well done," answered the neighbor.

And there, on the soil of Indiana, Abraham Lincoln wrote his name, with a stick, in large characters, — a sort of prophetic act, that students of history may love to ponder. For, since that day, he has "gone up higher," and written his name, by public acts, on the annals of every State in the Union.

The manner in which Abraham made progress in penmanship, writing on slabs and trees, on the ground and in the snow, anywhere that he could find a place, reminds us forcibly of Pascal, who demonstrated the first thirty-two propositions of Euclid in his boyhood, without the aid of a teacher. Bent upon gratifying his taste in this direction, he covered the walls of his play-room with geometrical figures, drawn with a piece of charcoal. The barn-door was sometimes his blackboard, and the ground itself often served him a good purpose, in the absence of something better.

In like manner David Wilkie, who became the renowned portrait-painter, learned to wield a blackened heather-stem with the skill of a veteran artist. In the absence of brush and pencil, he would snatch a half-burnt stick from the fire, and draw capital portraits of friends upon the nursery walls and other places. He became so absorbed in acquiring the art, that no obstacles could deter him. A piece of chalk, or a charred stick, and a board, sufficed about as well as brush and canvas.

Thus boys who are destined to become men of genius and power are wont to work their way up higher by dint of perseverance. They do what they undertake. They know no such word as fail. Success is their motto and rule of life. So it was with Abraham. Hitherto we have seen that he mastered every book put into his hand, and his subsequent career we shall find to be equally distinguished in this respect. As he acquired the art of writing with the smallest facilities, so he made all those acquisitions that will appear in subsequent pages with the poorest advantages. His pursuit of knowledge was under difficulties indeed!

XII.

THE LETTER AND VISITOR.

"NOW, Abe, you must write a letter for me to Parson Elkins," said his father, some eight or nine months after Mrs. Lincoln died, when Abraham had become a very good penman.

"What shall I write?" he inquired.

"Write about the death of your mother. He knows nothin' about it yet; and I want to ask him to visit us, and preach a funeral sermon."

"When shall he come?"

"When he can, I s'pose. He 'll take his own time for it; though I hope he 'll come soon."

"Perhaps he 's dead," added Abraham.

"What makes you think so?"

"He 's likely to die as mother, ain't he? and he may be dead when we don't know it, the same as she 's dead when he don't know it."

"Well, there 's somethin' in that," answered his father, smiling at the aforesaid reason. "Come, now, there 's some paper all ready for it, and I 'll tell you what to write."

Abraham made ready to pen the letter, and his

father proceeded to dictate the same. He directed him to write about the death of Mrs. Lincoln, when it occurred, and under what circumstances, and to invite him to visit them, and preach a funeral sermon. He also gave a description of their new home, and their journey thither, and wrote of their future prospects. Nor did he fail to mention that he had not regretted for a moment the exchange he made of a Slave State for a Free State.

"Now read it over," said Mr. Lincoln.

"The whole of it?"

"Of course; I want to hear it all. I may think of somethin' else by that time."

Abraham commenced to read it, while his father sat the very picture of satisfaction. There was genuine happiness to him in having his son prepared to write a letter. Never before had there been a member of his family who could perform this feat. It was a memorable event to him.

"See how much it is wuth to be able to write," said he, as Abraham finished reading the letter. "It's wuth ten times as much as it cost to be able to write only that one letter."

"It ain't much work to learn to write," said Abraham; "I'd work as hard again for it before I'd give it up."

"You'd have to give it up, if you was knocked about as I was when a boy."

"I know that."

THE FIRST LETTER.

"You don't know it as I do; and I hope you never will. But it's wuth more than the best farm to know how to write a letter as well as that."

"I shall write one better than that yet," said Abraham. "But how long will it take for the letter to go to Parson Elkins?"

"That's more than I can tell; but it will go there some time, and I hope it will bring him here."

"He won't want to come so far as this," said Abraham.

"It ain't so far for him as it was for us."

"Why ain't it?"

"Because he lives nearer the line of Indiana than we did. It ain't more than seventy-five miles for him to come, and he often rides as far as that."

The letter went on its errand, and Abraham was impatient to learn the result. On the whole, it was rather an important event in his young life, — the writing of that first letter. Was it strange that he should query whether it would reach the good minister to whom it was sent? Would it be strange if the writing of it proved one of the happy influences that started him off upon a career of usefulness and fame? We shall see.

Mr. Lincoln had much to say to his neighbors about the letter that his son had written, and they had much to say to him. It was considered remarkable for a boy of his age to do such a thing Not one quarter of the adults in all that region could write; and this fact rendered the ability of the boy in this regard all the more marvellous. It was noised abroad, and the result was, that Abraham had frequent applications from the neighbors to write letters for them. Nor was he indisposed to gratify their wishes. One of his traits of character was a generous disposition to assist others, and it prompted him to yield to their wishes in writing letters for them. Nor was it burdensome to him, but the opposite. He delighted to do it. And thus, as a consequence of his acquiring the art of penmanship, far-distant and long-absent friends of the pioneer families heard from their loved ones.

The letter brought the Parson. After the lapse of about three months he came. The letter reached him in Kentucky, after considerable delay, and he embraced the first opportunity to visit his old friends. Abraham had almost concluded that his letter was lost, as the favorite minister did not come. But one day, when the lad was about two miles from home, who should he see coming but Parson Elkins, on his old bay horse! He recognized him at once, and was delighted to see him.

"Why, Abe, is that you?" exclaimed the Parson. "Am I so near your home?"

"Yes, sir; did you get my letter?" Abraham

thought of the memorable letter the first thing. He had good evidence before him that the letter reached its destination, but he would know certainly.

"Your letter!" exclaimed Parson Elkins, inquiringly. "I got your father's letter." Abraham did not stop to think that the letter went in his father's name.

"I wrote it," he said.

"*You* wrote it! Is that so?"

"Yes, sir; father can't write, you know."

"O yes; I do remember now that he could n't write; and so you did it? And how did you learn to write? Not many boys that can write like that."

"Dennis showed me how, and that was the first letter I ever wrote."

"Better still is that, — the first one? Well, you need n't be ashamed of that."

They were advancing towards the cabin during this conversation, Abraham running alongside of the horse, and the Parson looking kindly upon him.

"There 's our house!" exclaimed Abraham, as they came in sight of it. "We live there," pointing with his finger.

"Ah! that 's a pleasant place to live. And there 's your father, I think, too."

"Yes, that 's him. He 'll be glad to see you."

"And I shall be glad to see him."

By this time they came near Mr. Lincoln, who recognized Parson Elkins, and gave him a most cordial greeting. He was really taken by surprise, although he had not relinquished all expectation of the Parson's coming.

"You find me in a lonely condition," said Mr. Lincoln. "Death has made a great change in my family."

"Very great indeed," responded Mr. Elkins. "I know how great your loss is; but I trust that the Lord sustains you. 'Whom the Lord loveth, he chasteneth.'"

"Yes; and I've wanted to see you more than anybody else in this trial."

"And how did she die? As she lived, I suppose?"

"O yes. She was as calm and happy in dying as she had been in living."

"And your loss is her gain."

"I've no doubt of that, — not at all."

"Nobody can have any doubts of it."

"Now, let me say, that, while you are here, I want you should preach a funeral sermon. You know all about my wife. You will stay over next Sunday, won't you?" It was now Wednesday.

"Why, yes, I can stay as long as that, though I must be about my Master's work."

"You will be about your Master's work, if you stay and preach a funeral sermon; and it may do a great sight of good."

"Very true; and I shall be glad to stay; for if

any one ever deserved a funeral sermon, it is your wife. But where shall I preach it ?"

"At her grave. I've had that arranged in my mind for a long time; and we'll notify the people; there will be a large attendance. The people thought a deal of her here."

It was arrranged that Mr. Elkins should preach the funeral sermon at the grave of Mrs. Lincoln on the following Sabbath. Accordingly notice was sent abroad to the distance of twelve or fifteen miles, and a platform was erected near the grave. Every preparation was made for the solemn event. Although a whole year had elapsed since Mrs. Lincoln died, yet a sermon to her memory was no less interesting to her surviving friends.

In the mean time, Mr. Elkins busied himself in intercourse with the family; and he visited some of the neighbors, and conversed with them on spiritual things. Abraham, too, received his special attention. The boy had improved rapidly since he left Kentucky, and his remarkable precocity was suited to draw the attention of such a preacher.

"You've found out what a pioneer boy is, I suppose, Abe," he said, alluding to his pleasant conversation with him on the subject in Kentucky.

"Yes, sir," replied the boy; "father was telling Mr. Turnham of it the other day," meaning that his father spoke of Mr. Elkins's conversation with his boy to the aforesaid neighbor.

"Well, I trust you 've proved yourself a pretty good one. You like to read and write, do you?"

"Yes, sir, the best of anything."

"Well, that hardly belongs to a pioneer boy. Very few of them can read and write. Living in the woods is not calculated to improve one in this respect. It may be that you won't always live in the woods, however."

"So father says; but I don't see how we can live anywhere else now."

"The Lord will provide a way perhaps. He took Moses out of the river to lead the children of Israel."

"Moses lived in the king's palace, did n't he?"

"Yes; but he was n't born there."

"He went to school there," added Abraham.

"Ah!" I see that you are familiar with the Bible; and this you owe to your blessed mother. Dear soul! Would that she could have lived to teach and guide you up to manhood!"

Abraham's eye grew tearful at these words; for they revived the memory of his excellent mother.

The Sabbath arrived,—a bright, beautiful day. From a distance of twelve or fifteen miles, the settlers came to listen to the sermon. Entire families assembled, parents and children, from the oldest to the youngest. Hoary age and helpless childhood were there. They came in carts, on horseback, and on foot, any way to get there. As they had preaching only when one of these pioneer preachers visited that vicinity, it was a treat to most of the inhabitants, and they manifested their interest by a general turn-out. The present occasion, however, was an unusual one, as the funeral sermon of Mrs. Lincoln was to be preached.

Parson Elkins was an earnest man, and the occasion inspired him with unusual fervor. None of the people had ever listened to him before, except the Lincoln family, and they were delighted with his services. His tribute to the memory of Mrs. Lincoln was considered just and excellent. None thought that too much was said in her praise. On the other hand, the general feeling was, rather, as one of the number expressed it, that, "say what he might in praise of her, he could n't say too much."

Abraham was deeply interested in the sermon, and it brought all of his mother's tenderness and love afresh to his mind. To him it was almost like attending her funeral over again. Her silent dust was within a few feet of him, and vivid recollection of her exceeding worth was in his heart. Was it strange that tears came unbidden to his eye? that his heart heaved with emotion that he vainly strove to conceal? No! A boy of such filial love, and noble, generous nature, could not suppress the deep feelings of his heart.

He drank in the sentiments of the discourse, too. He usually did this, as he was accustomed to think for himself. Often he criticised the sermons to which he listened, much to the amusement of those with whom he conversed. He sometimes called in question the doctrines preached. This was one of the things in which his prococity appeared. It was at this point that his mental activity and power was often seen. But the sentiments of the aforesaid funeral sermon especially impressed his mind.

"Don't the Bible say that the body returns to dust?" he inquired, on that Sabbath evening, as he sat thoughtfully in the cabin. His inquiry was addressed to his father, though Mr. Elkins was present.

"Yes; and the soul to God who gave it," answered his father.

"Then how can the body rise?" The preacher had represented his sainted mother's body as rising from that solitary spot on the resurrection morn.

"Mr. Elkins will tell you that," his father replied.

Abraham looked towards the preacher for an an swer.

"That 's worth thinking of," said Mr. Elkins; "and I 'm glad to see that you think about these things. Many boys let it go into one ear and out of the other. You don't see how the body that returns to dust can rise?"

"No, sir; if it turns to dust, it ain't a body any more."

"But God can bring together every particle of that body again, if he chooses, and make it rise, can't he?"

"How?" was Abraham's only answer. He could not understand it.

"That 's more than I can tell; but all things are possible with God; and the Bible says that the body will rise at the last day, and we ought to believe it, should n't we?"

"Yes, sir, if the Bible says so." Abraham could not question the truth of the Bible after the maternal lessons he had enjoyed.

"We can't fully understand everything that is true," continued the preacher. "I don't know how the grass grows, but it grows for all that."

Abraham looked puzzled. He was a very inquisitive boy, and was always putting questions about the reason of things. He wanted to understand everything to which he gave his attention. For this reason, as we shall see, he mastered every study to which he attended, whether he had a teacher or not. This desire to know why things are so and so is the secret of success to men who make their mark. It serves to make them think and investigate. It was so with Abraham, and he did not like to dispose of any subject by saying that it could not be understood. Hence he looked perplexed and unsatisfied.

This is but one instance of his precocious inquiries upon difficult subjects. Many might be cited, showing that his active brain busied itself upon subjects that were pressed upon his attention. In his reading the same thing was manifest. He talked about the subject-matter of the books he read, criticised them, and expressed his views freely. From the time he read Pilgrim's Progress to his manhood, this was true of him. In this respect he was unlike most boys, who are superficial in their views of things. They read, and that is the end of it. They think no more about it, — at least, they do not inquire into the *why* and *wherefore* of matters stated; and so the habit of sliding over things loosely is formed. They do not think for themselves. They accept things as true, because others say they are true. They are satisfied with knowing that things *are*, without asking *why* they are. But Abraham was not so. He thought, reflected; and this developed his mental powers faster than even school could do it.

The reader should understand more about these pioneer preachers, in order to appreciate the influences that formed Abraham's character, and therefore we will stop here to give some account of them.

They were not generally men of learning and culture, though some of them were men of talents. Few, if any of them, were ever in college, and some of them were never in school. But they had a call to preach, as they believed, and good and true hearts for doing it. Many of them preached almost every day, travelling from place to place on horseback, studying their sermons in the saddle, and carrying about with them all, the library they had in their saddle-bags. They stopped where night overtook them, and it was sometimes miles away from any human habitation, with no bed but the earth, and no covering but the canopy of heaven. They labored without a salary, and were often poorly clothed and scantily fed, being constrained to preach by the love of Christ. The following account of two pioneer preachers, by Milburn, will give the reader a better idea of this class of useful men than any description of ours, and it will be read with interest.

"One of these preachers, who travelled all through the Northwestern Territory, 'a tall, slender, graceful' man, 'with a winning countenance and kindly eye,' greatly beloved by all to whom he ministered, was presented by a large landholder with a title-deed of three hundred and twenty acres. The preacher was extremely poor, and there had been many times when he received scarcely enough support to keep soul and body together. Yet he labored on, and did much good. He seemed pleased with his present of land, and went on his way with a grateful heart. But in three months he returned, and met his benefactor at the door, saying, 'Here, sir, I want to give you back your title-deed.'

"'What's the matter?' said his friend, surprised. 'Any flaw in it?'

"'No.'

"'Is n't it good land?'

"'Good as any in the State.'

"'Sickly situation?'

"'Healthy as any other.'

"'Do you think I repent my gift?'

"'I have n't the slightest reason to doubt your generosity.'

"'Why don't you keep it, then?'

"'Well, sir,' said the preacher, 'you know I am very fond of singing, and there 's one hymn in my book the singing of which is one of the greatest comforts of my life. I have not been able to sing it with my whole heart since I was here. A part of it runs in this way: —

"No foot of land do I possess,
No cottage in the wilderness;
A poor wayfaring man,
I lodge awhile in tents below,
And gladly wander to and fro,
Till I my Canaan gain;
There is my house and portion fair,
My treasure and my heart are there,
And my abiding home."

"'Take your title-deed,' he added; 'I had rather sing that hymn with a clear conscience than own America.'

"There was another preacher of the pioneer class so intent upon his work that hunger and nakedness did not affright him. He was more scholarly than most of the preachers around him, and often sat up half the night, at the cabins of the hunters wnere he stopped, to study. These cabins were about twelve by fourteen feet, and furnished accommodations for the family, sometimes numbering ten or twelve children; and, as the forests abounded in '*varmints*,' the hens and chickens were taken in for safe keeping. Here, after the family retired, he would light a pine knot, 'stick it up in one corner of the huge fireplace, lay himself down on the flat of his stomach in the ashes,' and study till far into the night.

"Many a time was the bare, bleak mountain-side his bed, the wolves yelling a horrid chorus in his ears. Sometimes he was fortunate enough to find a hollow log, within whose cavity he inserted his body, and found it a good protection from the rain or frost.

"Once, seated at the puncheon dinner-table with a hunter's family, the party is startled by affrighted screams from the door-yard. Rushing out, they behold a great wildcat bearing off the youngest child. Seizing a rifle from the pegs over the door, the preacher raises it to his shoulder, casts a rapid glance along the barrel, and delivers his fire. The aim has been unerring, but too late, — the child is dead, already destroyed by the fierce animal.

"That same year he had a hand-to-hand fight with a bear, from which conflict he came forth victor, his knife entering the vitals of the creature just as he was about to be enfolded in the fatal hug.

"Often he emerged from the wintry stream, his garments glittering in the clear, cold sunlight, as if they had been of burnished steel armor, chill as the touch of death. During that twelvemonth, in the midst of such scenes, he travelled on foot and horseback *four thousand miles*, *preached four hundred times*, and found, on casting up the receipts, — yarn socks, woollen vests, cotton shirts, and a little silver change, — that his salary amounted to *twelve dollars and ten cents.*

"Yet he persevered, grew in knowledge and influence, became a doctor of divinity, and finally was made president of a university. He is known on the page of history as Henry Bidleman Bascom."

Such were the pioneer preachers of the West; of simple-hearted piety, lofty faith, a fiery zeal, unwavering fortitude, and a practical turn of mind, through which they did a great work for God.

We have made this digression from the thread of our story, to show what influences of the ministry were thrown around Abraham's early life. It is true the preachers to whom he listened were not "circuit-riders," as travelling preachers were called. They were Baptist ministers, who lived within twenty miles, and who occasionally preached in that neighborhood. During the first few years of Abraham's residence in Indiana, there was one Jeremiah Cash who sometimes preached in the vicinity, and the young listener became much interested in him. A few years later, two others came to that section of country to live. Their names were John Richardson and Young Lamar. One of them dwelt seven or eight miles from Abraham's home on the north, and the other eight or ten miles to the south ; and both of them were wont to preach at Mr. Lincoln's cabin, and at other cabins, as they had opportunity. Sometimes they preached in the open air, as Mr. Elkins did the funeral sermon. This was always the case when more people attended than could crowd into a log-house.

Such was all the pulpit influence that reached the boyhood and youth of Abraham. Yet it left indelible impressions upon his mind. Though it was small and inconstant, apparently, in comparison with the pulpit advantages that boys enjoy at the present day, it imbued his soul with sentiments that were never obliterated. He was much indebted to the unpolished eloquence of those pioneer preachers, whose sterling piety caused them to proclaim the truth with fidelity and earnestness. This was one of the few influences that contributed to make him a remarkable man.

XIII.

AT SCHOOL AGAIN.

NEARLY a year more passed. The sermon by Parson Elkins had ceased to be a theme of conversation among the settlers. Abraham had continued to assist his father, and devote his leisure moments to reading and writing. Time that other boys would spend in play he employed in poring over books. If he had no new ones to peruse, he read his old ones.

In the mean time, also, his father married Mrs. Sally Johnston, of Elizabethtown, Kentucky. It was an event of great joy to Abraham, and he gave his step-mother a most cordial welcome. The thought of having the place of his departed mother filled in the family was the source of real pleasure to him. The long period of loneliness that had elapsed since his mother's death served to make him doubly value the presence of one who would fill her place well. He did not receive her as a stranger. He did not cherish the least suspicion that she would prove otherwise than a loving parent. He gave her his confidence at once, and she bestowed upon him such care and tender regard as only a thoughtful, pious, faithful mother would. A mutual good understanding and affection sprang up between them, and it was never interrupted. Abraham obeyed her with a true filial love, and she still survives to bear witness to his obedience, diligence, and truthfulness. He gave her just the place in his young heart that his own mother occupied, and he was made happy by this honorable course. Nor did he ever have occasion to repent of his acts in this respect, for she proved a worthy successor of her who had rested nearly two years from her labors. We shall know her in future pages only as his mother.

Boys are apt to take advantage of such circumstances, and claim greater liberties with step-mothers than they did with the mothers who bore them. Often they are less affectionate and obedient, and disposed to have their own way, as if a mother-in-law had less right to control them. But it was not so with Abraham. He received her as a mother, and loved and obeyed her as such. He was not more respectful to his own mother than he was to her.

His new mother saw at once that he was no common boy. She was struck with his intelligence, knowledge, and uprightness. She had never seen his like. Of course she could scarcely help being deeply interested in his welfare.

About this time, among the families that came into that region to settle, was that of Mr. Andrew

Crawford. He was a man of more culture than most of the settlers, and was able to teach reading, writing, and arithmetic as far as the Rule of Three. His abilities becoming known, Mr. Lincoln urged him to open a school in his cabin, and promised to send Abraham, to which the man assented.

"Another chance for you to go to school," said Mr. Lincoln to his son, on returning home.

"Where?"

"That man Crawford, who moved in a little while ago, will begin school in a week."

"Have you seen him?" inquired Abraham.

"Yes, and he knows a great sight more than Hazel. He can learn you to cipher."

"He can?" and Abraham's reply indicated that he scarcely expected to see a man in that vicinity who could teach arithmetic.

"I can spare you some time now, and it will be a good chance for you to learn to cipher."

"When will he begin school?"

"Next week, no doubt; and two miles will be just far enough for you to walk to keep your legs limber."

"What shall I do for a book to cipher out of?"

"As to that, I can find one somewhere. I shall go to market before the week is out, and I'll see what I can find among the settlers there or on the way. I must have you study 'rithmetic somehow."

"A fine opportunity, Abe, for you to improve,"

added his mother, who liked the plan of his going to school. "I think you will like Mr. Crawford. He appears to be a nice man."

"That 's so," said his father; "I like Mr. Crawford much, what I 've seen of him. It 's a real blessin' to have such a man come here to live."

"Who else will go to school?" inquired Abraham.

"There 'll be as many as he wants. Mr. Turnham's boy will go, and Mr. Neale's girl, no doubt. Most all of the children can be spared now for a while."

"But some of 'em can't go, because they are too poor."

"That may be; but most on 'em can go if they 're a mind to."

Thus the way was opened for Abraham to attend school again, and preparations were made for the event. A new suit of clothes was made for him, as his old suit had become worn and ragged. It was not made of broadcloth or cassimere, as boys' clothes are now, but of "dressed buckskin," a very durable article. What it lacked in beauty was made up in strength. His father found an old arithmetic, and purchased it for him. Also a new cap was made for him out of a raccoon-skin. At that day men and boys wore straw hats in summer and fur caps in winter. Mothers could easily provide their boys with fur caps, since the skins of animals could always be easily obtained. Thus prepared, Abraham went to Mr. Crawford's school.

One Monday morning, as the scholars assembled, and were having a frolic before school-hour, their conversation turned upon a sermon they heard Jeremiah Cash preach on the day before.

"I liked the sermon the best of any I ever heard him preach," said Abraham. It was from the text, "So they took up Jonah, and cast him forth into the sea; and the sea ceased from her raging." (Jonah i. 15.)

"He put it on to Jonah," said David Turnham, with a laugh.

"And everybody else who don't do right," answered Abraham. "I can say half of his sermon now."

"You can't," replied David.

"I know I can, and if you don't believe it, I'll try."

"Try, then," added David. "Get on that stump, and let us have a preach," and he pointed to a large stump a rod distant.

"You think I can't do it," continued Abraham; "but I'll let you know that I can." So he mounted the stump and began the sermon. He gave the text, and proceeded to expound the truth, much to the merriment of the boys. He repeated the several heads correctly, and actually rehearsed a good part of the sermon.

"Well done, Abe!" exclaimed one of the boys; "that's what nobody else can do. You can preach it next Sunday, if you're a mind to."

"I'll come and hear you," said David.

"And so will I," added another.

"And I too," still another.

After this, Abraham often repeated portions of sermons to which he had listened, just to gratify his companions. He possessed a retentive memory, and, what was better, he was a very close listener. An active mind like his is likely to appropriate what it hears, especially when its thirst for knowledge is so great. His habit of close attention had quite as much to do with his ability to repeat portions of sermons as his retentive memory. The young are too apt to be listless, inattentive in the house of God. They recollect little of the sermons they hear, because they do not give heed thereto. Let them listen as Abraham did, and become absorbed in the sermon, and they will be able to appropriate much of what they hear.

Mr. Crawford, from the door of his cabin, heard Abraham in the above effort, and he was truly surprised. He had seen enough of the lad before to become impressed with his abilities, but this boyish act won his admiration. He thought it was remarkable. He had never seen a boy who could do that before. He did not think that another boy could do it as well.

The celebrated Dr. Chalmers carried this matter further still in his boyhood. He would not only repeat portions of sermons to which he listened in the presence of his mates, but he would even select a text, and discourse from it when standing in a chair. He was not more than nine years of age when he did this.

One of the most distinguished of English statesmen was still more remarkable in his boyhood for the ability to repeat sermons that he heard. At eight years of age, his father would stand him upon the table, and require him to repeat the sermon that he heard on the day before, and he would do it with considerable accuracy.

It is interesting to note what similarity in such things there is among the men who have made their mark in the world. Whatever calling of life they have chosen, there are certain elements of success that are traceable even back to their childhood.

But we were to speak of the school. Some eight or ten children attended, and Abraham gave special attention to arithmetic. He did not neglect reading and writing, but continued to attend to those branches. His whole heart was in his school, and his advancement was rapid.

"Abe is a wonderful boy," said Crawford to Mr. Lincoln one day. "He is never satisfied without knowing all about his lessons."

"He has been so all his days," replied his father.

"He wants to know everything that anybody else does, and he don't see why he can't."

"That 's it. I 've been surprised to see what pluck he has to master a lesson."

"As to that, he 's just so about everything else. He does what I set him about, if it 's ever so hard."

"I don't doubt it," continued Crawford. "I was pleased yesterday to see him work out a sum. He could n't do it for a long time, and he asked me one or two questions about it, and I answered him, and then let him work. He tugged away at it until he mastered it, and a happier boy I never saw."

"He told me about it last night, for he studies his arithmetic every night, and would rather keep at it than to go to bed, generally."

"What a boy!" continued Mr. Crawford. "He ought to have a better chance than a backwoods life can afford him. And he seems to be as good as he is bright."

"Yes; he 's a very good boy. We can't expect boys will do everything right, you know; but he 's good to mind, generally. His mother thinks there never was such a boy, to obey her." And this last testimony was a confirmation of what we have said of his filial love and obedience.

"I was struck with his honesty the other day," added Mr. Crawford. "I saw that a buck's horn, that was nailed up on the back side of our house, was broken off, and I concluded that some of the boys did it. So I asked them the next day, when they had all got still, who of them broke it, and Abe answered promptly, " I did it."

" Just like him," said his father.

" I said, how happened that, Abe ? "

" I did n't mean to do it," he replied. " I hung on it, and it broke. I should n't have done it if I had thought it would break."

" I dare say he spoke the truth," said his father.

" I have no doubt of it ; but few boys would own up like that. Most boys would try to conceal what they had done, and would n't own it till they were obliged to."

" That 's so ; and I 've thought that it might be owing a little to the Life of Washington that he read some time ago. He seemed to think a sight of his owning up that he cut the cherry-tree with his new hatchet ; and he spoke of it ever so many times."

" Well, this was certainly like that," said Mr. Crawford ; " and I took occasion to say that it was a noble trait to confess a wrong that was done, instead of trying to conceal it."

" He never was disposed to conceal his wrong-doings. He takes all the blame to himself, and don't try to put it on to anybody else."

" I should think so ; and such truthfulness is worthy of all praise," said Mr. Crawford.

Whatever Mr. Lincoln may have thought about the Life of Washington influencing his boy, there can be no doubt that such an exhibition of character as the above was the fruit of maternal instruction. The reader will remember those Sabbath lessons of which we spoke, when the Bible was made the text-book at the fireside, and the ninth commandment was impressed upon the mind of Abraham with seriousness. That was the time, doubtless, when truthfulness as a principle of action was rooted in his soul.

One day, on returning from school, his father said to him: "I 've seen Mr. Wood to-day, and he wants you should write a letter for him to send 'way off to Massachusetts. He 's got friends there."

"When?" asked Abraham.

"To-night he 'll be over here, and tell you what he wants to have you write."

"Then I 'll study my arithmetic before he comes. It 's real hard now."

"So much the better, if you can master it."

"So Mr. Crawford says."

"Yes; I know what he thinks, for I have talked with him about it. He knows what is best for you and all the rest of the boys. But you must go at your lesson, if you mean to study before Mr. Wood comes."

Winter had now set in, and the cold was quite

severe. An extra fire was made up for the evening by piling on huge logs. The reader will recollect that we said lamps were out of the question with the poor settlers. Nor were they needed, since a large fire of logs, four feet in length, would light up the cabin better than a dozen lamps. On the evening in question the log-house was filled with a blaze of light from the fire, to enable Abraham to write the aforesaid letter with ease.

Thus his acquisitions were brought into use at once, particularly his skill in the art of penmanship. As we have said before, he wrote letters for the neighborhood. He became the scribe of a number of families, and made himself extremely useful. He received his own reward, too, in the facility which it afforded him to express his thoughts in after years. Says another of him, in this particular: "That he was selected for this purpose was doubtless owing not more to his proficiency in writing than to his ability to express the wishes and feelings of those for whom he wrote in clear and forcible language, and to that obliging disposition that has always distinguished him in subsequent life. It cannot be doubted that something of Mr. Lincoln's style and facility of composition in later years, both as a writer and speaker, is to be traced back to these earlier efforts as an amanuensis for the neighborhood."

XIV.

STILL AT SCHOOL.

"YOU 'LL keep on at school," said Mr. Lincoln to him. "I 've seen Mr. Crawford, and you 'll go awhile longer." He had been to school eight or ten weeks at that time.

"I 'm glad of that," said Abraham; "I want to keep on with my arithmetic, and Mr. Crawford wants to have me."

"Well, the matter is fixed, and you 'll go. In the spring I shall want your help, and then you 'll have to stop."

"How long will it be before that?"

"Only a few weeks, and you must make the most of it."

"Perhaps this will be your last opportunity," said his mother, who stood by.

"More 'n 'as likely as not," added his father. "And you 'll soon know as much about 'rithmetic as Mr. Crawford; and as to writin' and readin', I s'pose you 're as well off as he is now."

"But, Abe, I want you should go to Mr. Neale's for me to-morrow morning, before you go to school," said his mother.

"What for?"

"I'll tell you when you get ready to go. I sha'n't want you to go if it rains. It looks some like raining."

"We boys were going to school early to-morrow, to have a play," he said, thus intimating that going upon an errand for her would interfere essentially with his plans.

"You will have times enough for play."

"Yes; but to-morrow morning we agreed to all come early to school, and the boys will all go."

"Well, you can go if you want to very much. I suppose that your play is more important than my business"; and this was said in a tone that indicated rebuke. Abraham received it in that light.

"No it ain't, mother," he said. "I shall go to Mr. Neale's for you, whether I play any or not."

"But the boys will be disappointed, you say?" and her tone indicated her meaning.

"That 's no matter. I shall do what you want to have me first, whether they like it or not. I shall go to Mr. Neale's for you in the morning." This was said with cheerfulness, as if he did not regret leaving his sports to obey his mother, nor was it a solitary instance. It was not uncommon for him to forego personal pleasure to gratify his parents. He was reared to do this. It was a part of that domestic culture to which he was subjected from his youth. He did it as a matter of course. He seldom manifested any of that sulkiness and rebellious spirit that is so common among boys when required to lay aside their plays for work. The command of his parents was high authority to him.

The morning dawned, and the errand was performed before going to school. As it turned out, however, he reached Mr. Crawford's house as soon as David Turnham, whom he overtook on his way. Obedience had not put him behindhand. It made him a little smarter than usual, so that he accomplished much in a little time. This is usually the case, as many facts prove.

"Hallo, David! I thought I should be the last one there," exclaimed Abraham, as he came in sight of his playmate.

"If you was the last one there, it would be the first time," was David's reply. "You are always on hand." And that was true. He was generally punctual on all occasions.

"I had to go to Mr. Neale's first this morning, or I should have been along before."

"We are soon enough now."

"What are the boys up to there?" asked Abraham, looking up as they drew near Mr. Crawford's, and seeing the scholars huddled together, as if intent on something.

"Sure enough!" was all David replied.

Coming up to the boys, they found a toad in the circle, with which they were amusing themselves.

"Don't," exclaimed Abraham, as one of the boys poked him with a stick.

"Don't what?" answered the lad, as with a punch he knocked the toad over.

"Don't treat him so," said Abraham. "How would you like to be poked about with a stick like that?"

"Try it, and see."

"Well, it is cruel to treat him so," added Abraham.

"Why, it 's nothin' but a toad."

"Don't toads have feeling?" asked Abraham.

"I don't know whether they do or not," answered the boy, giving the animal another thrust.

"You sha'n't do so," said Abraham, taking hold of the boy's arm.

"You 're a chicken-hearted feller, Abe, as ever lived. I should think the toad was your brother."

"Whether it is or not, there 's no use in abusing it."

"That 's it," said David, who stood looking on; "I go in for Abe. He would n't hurt a fly."

"He would if he trod on one," answered one of the number.

"He would n't tread on one a purpose," said David. A very true remark, for Abraham was known for his tenderness to animals. He could kill game for food as a necessity, and dangerous wild animals, but his soul shrunk from torturing even a fly.

Mr. Crawford had witnessed a part of this scêne from his cabin, and he came out at this stage of the affair, and rebuked the cruelty of the boys who were torturing the toad, while he commended Abraham for his tenderness. It was an additional act to exalt the latter in his estimation.

"We are coming to the Rule of Three now," said Mr. Crawford to Abraham, "and that will be all you can learn of me."

"Is it hard?" asked the boy.

"It won't be for you. I think you can get through it by the time your father wants you this spring."

"Why is it called the Rule of Three?"

"I hardly know. Some call it Simple Proportion, and that is the true name for it. You will see a reason for it, too, when you come to master it."

"What if I don't master it?"

"I'll risk you on that. It won't be of so much use to you as what you have been over already. Some people don't study it."

"My father never studied arithmetic," said Abraham.

"Nor mine. Not half the folks about here have studied it."

"Father never had a chance to study it when he was a boy.

"That's the case with a good many."

"Well, I can cipher now in Addition, Subtraction, Multiplication, and Division."

"Yes, you understand those rules well, and you will always find use for them."

So, encouraged by his instructor, who was a man of good sense, Abraham grappled with the so-called "Rule of Three." It was somewhat more difficult for him to comprehend this rule than it was the previous ones; yet he was not discouraged. His discriminating mind and patient labor did the work for him, and he enjoyed the happiness of understanding Proportion by the time his school-days were over. We do not mean that he comprehended it fully, so as to be complete master of it, but he understood it, as we are wont to say that pupils understand the rules they have been over at school. At least, he made such progress that he was prepared to become master of all the rules he had studied, by devoting his leisure moments to them thereafter.

We must stop here to relate one more incident of these school-days, because it illustrates a trait of character for which Abraham was well known in his youth. We often find the key to a boy's character by observing his intercourse with companions at school.

It was near the end of his term of school at Mr. Crawford's house. Several boys were on their way home at the close of school in company with Abraham, when a difficulty arose between two of them about spelling a word.

"You did n't spell it right," said John.

"Yes I did spell it right," replied Daniel. "I spelt it just as Mr. Crawford did."

"He said you did n't spell it so."

"I know he said so, but he did n't understand me. I spelt it just as he did."

"I know you did n't," continued John.

"And I know I did," retorted Daniel. "You are a liar, if you say so."

"Don't call me a liar!" exclaimed John, doubling up his fist. "You 'll get it, if you say that again!"

"I stump you to do it, old madpiece!" said Daniel, putting himself into an attitude of defiance.

"Come, Dan, don't," said Abraham, throwing one of his arms over his neck.

"Let him come, if he wants to," said John, in a great rage; "I 'll give it to him: he 's a great coward."

"What 's the use, John?" answered Abraham, throwing his other arm around John's shoulders, so as to bring himself between the two wrathy boys; "that ain't worth fighting about."

"Yes it is, too," answered John. "You would n't be called a liar by anybody I know, and I won't nuther." Abraham was now walking along between the two boys, with his arms over their shoulders.

"Yes I would, too; and I should n't care neither, if it was n't true."

"Nobody would think of calling you a liar," added John.

"They would n't call you so, if you did n't care anything about it," answered Abraham; and there was much truth in the remark.

By this time the two combatants had cooled off considerably, and Daniel put out the last spark of fire by adding, "I'll take it back, John."

"That's a good fellow," said Abraham, while John was mute. Five minutes thereafter the two vexed boys were on good terms, their difficulties having been adjusted by Abraham, "the peace-maker," as he was often called. He could not endure to see broils among his companions, and he often taxed all his kind feelings and ingenuity to settle them. This trait of character has been prominent through all his life. And last, though not least, we had an exhibition of it, when, at the outbreak of the rebellion in 1861, he put his arms around the neck of both North and South, and attempted to reconcile them. But his effort proved less successful than it did in the case of John and Daniel; for the Southern combatant was too far gone with madness to be persuaded.

With his knowledge of the Rule of Three closed Abraham's school-days. He never attended school more after going to Mr. Crawford. In all, he did not go to school more than six months in his life, and then he was under the charge of teachers so ignorant that they would not now be tolerated.

It should have been stated before, that, near the close of Mr. Crawford's school, Abraham's mother bought him a second-hand Life of Henry Clay, and it was to him a deeply interesting work. He read it over and over, and commented upon the character of Clay; and he grew up an admirer of "Old Harry of the West." There appears to have been some connection between that volume — the Life of Clay — and his political connections in after life, as he was ever known as a "Clay Whig." Thus it is that a single book may decide the political course of the reader through life.

Nearly two years after, he came into possession of a second Life of Washington in a manner so interesting, that we shall give a full account of it in the next chapter. His experience, in the mean time, continued to flow on in about the same way, so that we have no need of dwelling upon it; and therefore we shall proceed to narrate the aforesaid affair, that the reader may see the elements of character appearing therein.

XV.

A TRIAL AND TREASURE.

"THE greatest man that ever lived!" said Abraham, as he sat upon a log in the woods, conversing with David Turnham. "This country has a right to be proud of Washington."

"That is your opinion; but I guess the British won't say so," answered David.

"And that is just because they were whipped by him; and they don't want to own up."

"How do you know so much about Washington, Abe?"

"Because I have read about him, and I always heard that he made the red-coats run for life."

"Who do you mean by the red-coats?"

"Why, the British, to be sure. They were called 'red-coats,' because they wore coats of that color. I expect that they looked splendidly, though they did n't feel very splendidly, I guess, after they got whipped."

"Have you read the Life of Washington?"

"Of course I have, a good while ago. I read Weem's Life of Washington, and that shows that he was the greatest man who ever lived."

"Is that like the one Mr. Crawford has?"

"I did n't know that Mr. Crawford had a Life of Washington." He did not see it when he went to his school.

"Well, he has; for I heard him talking with father about it."

"How long ago?"

"Not more than two or three weeks ago."

"You don't know the name of the author? There are Lives of Washington written by different men."

"I don't remember who wrote this. I did n't mind much about what they were saying."

"I can find out," added Abraham; and he did find out. He embraced the first opportunity to inquire of a neighbor, and learned that it was Ramsay's Life of Washington that Mr. Crawford owned.

"Can I borrow it?" he inquired of his parents, for he was very anxious to read it.

"Perhaps he won't like to lend it," answered his mother.

"I shall find that out when I ask him," said Abraham.

"And you should tell him that you will not take it unless he is perfectly willing to let you have it."

"Then I may ask him, may I?"

"If you are very desirous to read it."

"Well, I am, and I will go there to-night when I get through work."

Abraham was elated with the idea of getting hold of this new work. He viewed the character of Washington with admiration, and he would know what different biographers said of him. He was not a little impatient for his day's work to be done. He toiled as usual, however, with a good degree of interest in his work, until night, when he prepared himself to call on Mr. Crawford.

The family gave him a cordial welcome, and Mrs. Crawford said: "I wonder what has brought you out to-night. I have n't seen you here for a long time."

"Perhaps you won't be so glad to see me after you learn what I came for," replied Abraham.

"And what did you come for, that makes you think so?" asked Mr. Crawford.

"I came to borrow a book."

"A book, hey! That is a good errand, I am sure."

"But I did not know as you would be willing to lend it."

"What book is it?" asked Mr. Crawford. "I have no doubt that I can accommodate you."

"It is Ramsay's Life of Washington. I was told that you had it, and I want to read it."

"I wish all the boys wanted to read it," said Mr. Crawford. "I will lend it to you, Abe, with great pleasure. I am glad to see that you like to read."

"I will not take it unless you are perfectly willing to lend it," said Abraham.

"If I did not want you should have it, I should tell you so. I am not one of those persons who is afraid to tell what he thinks. I am glad that I have the book to lend you."

"I will take good care of it, and return it to you all safe," responded Abraham. This was just like him. So considerate a boy would not ask the loan of a book without some diffidence, and when it is borrowed, he would feel that great care must be used to preserve it. He valued the few books which he himself possessed so highly, as to lead him to think that other people held their volumes in equal estimation. It was really an excellent trait of character that caused him to use so much discretion in borrowing books. For the borrowing of this single article has been the occasion of much trouble in neighborhoods. In consequence of thoughtlessness and less regard for the interests of others than their own, many persons have borrowed books and never returned them, or else returned them in a much worse condition than when they were received. Frequently books are lost in this way from Sabbath-school and other libraries. Borrowers do not return them. They think so little of their obligations, that the books are forgotten and lost. Book-borrowers are very apt to be negligent, so that when we see a lad so particular as Abraham was, it is worth while to take note of the fact.

"It will take me some time to read so large a

work," said he, as he took it from Mr. Crawford. "Perhaps you will want it before I get through with it."

"O no; you are such a great reader that you will finish it in short metre. Keep it as long as you want it, and I shall be suited."

"I thank you," Abraham replied, as he arose to leave. "Good night."

"Good night," several voices responded.

It was a very joyful evening to Abraham as he bore that Life of Washington home, and sat down about the middle of the evening to read the first chapter therein.

"Keep it nice," said his mother. "Remember that it is a borrowed book."

"I will try," he replied. "Mr. Crawford was perfectly willing to lend it, and I shall be none the less careful on that account."

Those were pleasant hours of leisure that he devoted to reading Ramsay's Life of Washington. Every evening, after his day's labor was completed, he read the work with absorbing interest, and at other times when he could find a spare moment it was in his hand. He had nearly completed it, when the following mishap caused him many unpleasant thoughts and feelings.

A driving storm was raging, so that he could perform little labor except what could be done under cover. Of course his book was in his hand much of the time, and the whole of the dreary evening, to a late hour, it was his companion. On going to bed, he laid it down directly under a large crack between the logs, and the wind changing in the course of the night, the rain was driven into the house, and the book was wet through. The first sight that met Abraham's eye in the morning was the drenched book, and his feelings can be better imagined than described.

"O dear!" he exclaimed. "That book is spoiled!" And he could scarcely restrain the tears that welled up to his eyes.

"How did you happen to lay it there?" asked his mother.

"I never thought about its raining in there. But only look at it! it is completely soaked!" and he lifted it up carefully to show his mother.

"O, I am so sorry! it is ruined!" she said.

"I can dry it," answered Abraham, "but that will not leave it decent. See! the cover will drop off, and there is no help for it. What will Mr. Crawford say? I told him that I would keep it very carefully, and return it to him uninjured."

"Well, it is done, and can't be helped now," added his mother; "and I have no doubt that you can fix it with Mr. Crawford."

"I have no money to pay him for it, and I don't see how I can make it good to him."

"Perhaps he can suggest a way," said his mother.

"He ought to be paid for it."

"Of course he had, and he may want you to do some work for him, which will be the same as money to him. You 'd better take the book to him to-day, and see what you can do."

"I am almost ashamed to go. He will think that I am a careless fellow."

"Never be ashamed to do right, my son."

"I am not ashamed to do right. I was only saying how I felt. I told him that I would keep it nicely."

"And so you meant to; but accidents will happen sometimes, if we are careful."

"He shall be paid for it somehow," continued Abraham. "I will see him to-day."

The volume was exposed to the heat of the fire that day, and when Abraham was ready to go to Mr. Crawford's in the evening, it was dry enough for transportation. The storm had passed away, and the stars were looking down from the skies, as he took the book, carefully wrapped in a cotton handkerchief, and proceeded to Mr. Crawford's. His heart was heavy and sad, and he dreaded to open the subject to him.

"Good evening, Abe! Got through with the book so quick?" said Mr. Crawford.

"Good evening," responded Abraham, in his usual manly way. "I have brought the book back, although I have not finished it."

"Keep it, then, keep it, then," exclaimed Mr. Crawford, before the lad could tell his story. "I told you to keep it as long as you wanted it."

"Perhaps you won't want I should keep it longer when you hear what has happened to it." And he proceeded to untie the handkerchief in which it was wrapped.

"I should think you had a lot of jewels there by the manner you carry it," said Mr. Crawford, smiling.

"There," said Abraham, taking out the book, "it is ruined. I laid it down last night where the rain beat in and wet it through, and it is spoiled. I am very sorry, indeed, and want to pay you for it in some way."

"Pretty well used up," said Mr. Crawford, taking up the book. "Yes, I see that it is a little worse for the wear. And you had n't read it through?"

"No, sir; I had some forty or fifty pages more to read."

"You can read that yet: there is enough left of it for that," and Mr. Crawford showed by his jovial air that he did not feel so badly as the borrower did.

"But now I have ruined the book, I want to pay you for it in some way. Have you any work for me to do?"

"Plenty of it: always have work enough on hand for two or three smart fellows to do."

"How much was the book worth?" asked Abraham.

"I hardly know. Do you want to pay me the full value of it, and keep it for your own."

"Yes, I should like that, though I had not thought of that way."

"Well, what kind of work do you want to do?"

"Anything that I can do to suit you."

"Well, I tell you what it is, Abe, I'm in great trouble about my corn. You see the whole of my corn has been stripped of the blades as high as the ear, and is now all ready to have the tops cut off for winter fodder; but my hands are full of other work, and how it is to be done is more than I can tell. Now if you can help me out of this scrape, we can square the account about the book. What do you say to that?"

"I say that I am willing to do that, or anything else that suits you."

"You are very accommodating, but you won't lose anything on that account. How much of my field of corn will you cut, and keep the book for your own?"

"You mean the field of corn over yonder?" pointing to the eastward.

"Yes, you know just where it is. That is all the corn I have."

"I will cut the whole of it for the book," replied Abraham, as if conscious that it was a magnanimous offer to repair the damage he had done.

"Agreed," answered Mr. Crawford; "and a very generous offer, too. I will not require you to do so much for the book, unless you choose to do it."

"I choose to do it."

"When will you begin?"

"To-morrow morning; the sooner I pay for the book, the better."

"Come on, then, bright and early, and the book is yours."

Abraham rose to go out, when Mr. Crawford said: "You may take the book to-night, if you wish."

"It will be time enough to take the book when I have paid for it," replied Abraham, with a smile playing over his face. And he left without taking it.

After he had gone, Mr. and Mrs. Crawford discussed the matter freely, and exchanged views respecting the character of the boy, as they often did when he was a scholar in their house.

"He is one of a thousand," said Mrs. Crawford; "so honest and manly!"

"All of that," responded her husband. "It would be difficult to find a boy of his age who would want to read the Life of Washington, and much more, to pay for it by hard labor."

"That is a fact," said Mrs. Crawford. "I have often thought that he was different from all the rest of the boys. He knows so much, and seems altogether beyond his years!"

"A great comfort to his father and mother," added Mr. Crawford, yawning, and throwing his head back in his chair for a nap. "He 'll make something, if he lives."

"And be greatly missed if he don't live," responded his wife. "His father thinks a deal of him; and who can blame him for it?"

Abraham went home with a much lighter heart. The injury to the book was settled without implicating his character for honesty and carefulness. Indeed, it was settled in a manner that rather developed the noble qualities of his heart. His success was announced at once to his parents, and the arrangement into which he had entered to pay for the book.

"Cheap enough," said his father. "If you can make good such an injury and get the book, too, for three or four days' labor, it is cheap."

"And save your honor and character, too," added his mother. "That is worth more than all."

It was arranged that Abraham should stop with Mr. Crawford until his work was done, and the next morning he took an early start to fulfil his engagement. It was a bright, beautiful autumnal day, and his own heart was in sweet harmony with nature around him. Never did a toiler enter upon the most profitable piece of labor with more enthusiasm than he undertook to pay for the injured book.

We have not space to give his experience at Mr.

Crawford's in detail. Suffice to say, that it took him just three days to cut the corn, and they were three days of very hard labor most cheerfully performed. He had a pleasant time in the family, and their views of his character were more glowing than ever at the end of the time. They saw qualities of mind and heart in him which they had overlooked before.

When the work was done, he took his book and carried it home in triumph. It was to him one of the finest acquisitions he had made. He felt rich. His poverty was nothing. His humble home was as bright a spot as the Western world could boast. He had no money, but he owned another book, — Ramsay's Life of Washington, — and that was enough. It was a long-to-be-remembered day that made him the happy possessor of this work.

"A good bargain for both of you," said his father.

"It is a good one for me, I am certain of that," replied Abraham.

"Perhaps it is better for you than for him, because you are young, and need to read such a work for information. Every boy ought to know all about Washington, the 'Father of his Country.' You are a good reader, and you ought to be thankful for it. It is very hard not to know how to read. I would give almost anything if I could read as well as you can."

"Learn now, father," replied Abraham.

"It 's hard teaching old dogs new tricks," he answered jocosely. "I should n't make much headway now, I reckon."

"'Better late than never,' as mother says."

"Perhaps so; but there is not much need of my learning now, as you can read to me all I want."

"You won't always have me to read to you."

"What 's going to become of you so suddenly?"

"I shall have to work out for a living, and it won't be long neither before I shall be able to do it."

"I 'm glad to see that you are thinking about it. In these times there is no room for idlers. In fact, that is true at all times; God helps only those who help themselves."

"Those are all who ought to be helped," said Abraham.

"That is so; and I hope that you will always have such industrious habits that the blessing of God will rest upon you."

The reader can but admire the true manliness with which Abraham settled the book affair. There was no attempt to evade responsibility in the matter, no effort at concealment, no seeking to excuse himself, but a manly statement of the whole affair, with a noble, generous offer to repair the injury in full. Many boys would falter in such circumstances, and try to manufacture some defence for their course, and be totally unwilling to labor half so long to square an account. Such manhood and uprightness is rare in boys of thirteen or fourteen years of age. His prompt, conscientious course is an example to all the boys of our land who would win a good name for themselves, and share the approbation of Heaven.

XVI.

EIGHTEEN YEARS OLD.

WE pass to Abraham's eighteenth birthday. He was as tall as his father, and much stronger. He had labored constantly during the four years and more that had elapsed since the affair narrated in the last chapter occurred. Most of the time he had used the axe, cutting wood and splitting rails. Sometimes, however, he had labored a day or two at a time farming for his father and others. His father cultivated but a small farm, as he worked some at his trade, — that of a carpenter, — so that Abraham frequently labored for others in the woods. He excelled almost every one in the vicinity in the skilful use of the axe, and hence his labors were much sought.

This sort of labor developed his physical powers wonderfully, and he became remarkable for his endurance. He could weary out nearly every man with whom he worked.

At the same time, he had not neglected his mind. He borrowed books wherever he could, and read and re-read them. He had added two more volumes to his own possessions, also, and these were the Life of Franklin and Plutarch's Lives. And so his was not an inferior library. The Bible, Spelling-Book, Æsop's Fables, Pilgrim's Progress, Lives of Washington, Clay, and Franklin, together with Plutarch's Lives, are a library in themselves; just the books to impress an active mind like Abraham's, and develop its strong powers.

His reputation for industry, energy, perseverance, and honesty was fair as ever. He was just as much devoted to his parents also as he was in his boyhood. And though he talked much of going away to seek his fortune, feeling that he ought to do better than he possibly could there, yet he yielded to the expressed desire of his parents, and remained at home.

Such was Abraham, and his condition, about the time he was eighteen years of age, when one day, in early winter, he was notified of a house-raising some six miles off. A new-comer desired to get up a shelter for his family as soon as possible. It had become customary for the settlers to turn out on such occasions, and put up a log-house for a man in a few hours. They sometimes went as far as ten miles to house-raisings and log-rollings.

"You must go, Abe," said David. "Nobody can lift any if you ain't there."

"Father has made all his arrangements to go to market to-morrow, and I don't know as I can leave."

"Yes you can," said his father, who overheard him. "You must go because I can't. I'm afraid that it will snow soon, and I must go to market to-morrow at any rate. I'm afraid to put it off another day. The hogs are all ready, and I promised them at this time."

Mr. Lincoln raised many hogs. They were let loose in the forests, where they fattened for the market, and then were killed and carried to the nearest market, situated on a creek, eighteen miles distant, emptying into the Ohio River, six miles above Rockport, near where the town of Grandview now stands.

"I should like to go to the raising," said Abraham; "but I did n't know that you would think it best, as you was going off."

"That makes no difference. You'll get back before it's very late. If I don't go soon to market, Nichols will think I don't keep my word."

It was the custom with the settlers to carry deer-skins, venison-hams, and various kinds of furs to market, to exchange for goods. Frequently, also, they obtained goods on credit, and promised pork, to be delivered late in the fall or early in the winter. This was the case with Mr. Lincoln. He had promised pork to pay his store-bill, and he would not disappoint the man. He had some furs to carry, also.

"Then I'll go, David," said Abraham. "What time will you start?"

"As early as you'll come along. It ain't best to keep them waiting, and they'll wait till you get there." This last remark was made in a complimentary manner, as Abraham was regarded a superior hand on such occasions, because of his great strength and readiness to do.

"I understand you," answered Abraham. "I take your words for all they are worth."

"And that ain't much, I s'pose you'll say," quickly responded David. "But come on in good season. It's something of a walk there?" And he left for home.

On the next day, Mr. Lincoln started with his load for market, and Abraham went to the raising.

We would say here, that Mr. Lincoln carried his pork to market on a "truck wagon," drawn by oxen. It was made by sawing wheels off a log two or three feet in diameter, and, having cut holes through the centre of the wheels, wooden axles were put into them and fastened with a wooden linchpin. Abraham frequently drove this team to market.

The house-raising affair proved to be a pleasant thing. There was a general attendance of the settlers, and the usual good feeling and cheerfulness in lending a helping hand. After the work was done, there was a mutual exchange of friendly greetings, according to the custom of those times, and various amusements were enjoyed. On this account it was far into the evening when the younger portion of the company separated for home.

Abraham, together with three or four companions, was returning, and had come within two miles of his home, when their progress was arrested by an unusual scene.

"What 's this?" cried David, just descrying some object before him. "Somebody's horse here!"

"Yes; and there 's his rider in the ditch," said Abraham, discovering a man lying in the mud and water.

"Who is it?" asked David, under great excitement. "Thrown off?" He supposed that an unruly horse had thrown his rider.

"No," replied Abraham, "more likely he fell off. The horse would n't be standing here if he was ugly, and had thrown him. Let 's see who it is." And he proceeded to pull him into the road, where they could have a view of his face.

"He 's drunk," said David, who began to suspect the cause of his being in the gutter.

"He 's drunk or dead,—there 's no doubt about that," added Abraham. "He would n't go to bed there, if he knew what he was about."

"It is old Myers, ain't it?" suggested one of the boys, getting a better view of his face. "It looks like him."

"Sure enough, it is," replied Abraham; "and that 's his old horse. I 've seen it forty times.

He 's drunk as he can be. He ain't dead, if it 's him. You can't kill him so easy."

"And his old horse is used to waiting for him on such occasions," said David. "But how do you suppose he came 'way off here at this time of night. It 's fifteen miles or more to his house."

"Before we find that out, we better see whether he is frozen or not," said Abraham. "His clothes are stiff as they can be."

"If he ain't frozen now, he would be before mornin'," added another boy. "Lucky for him that we came along."

The man proved to be Myers, who was an intemperate person living fifteen or sixteen miles distant; and he had fallen from his horse in a state of beastly intoxication.

"What shall we do with him?" asked David.

"There 's only one thing to do with him," answered Abraham. "We must carry him over to Mr. Dale's." That was the nearest house. "He 'll freeze to death here."

Mr. Dale's house was about one fourth of a mile back, and it was wise for them to go to the nearest place. The wretched man's condition required immediate action.

"Let us put him on his horse," continued Abraham, "we can't lug him over there. Get hold of the other side of him, boys, and we 'll lift him on the horse." And suiting his actions to his words, Abraham took hold of one arm, and putting his other hand under his shoulders, with the help of his companions, they raised him to his feet, and set him, or rather laid him, on his horse. One of the number led the animal, while the others held the drunken man on.

"He don't know what a good ride he 's having," said one of the boys, laughing.

"And so he 'll never thank us for it," added another.

"I don't think it 's any laughing matter," responded Abraham. "If it was your father, you would n't feel much like joking."

"That 's a fact," said David, who was wont to take a correct view of things. "The man is to be pitied, after all."

"His horse deserves an extra peck of oats for waitin' for him," suggested Daniel. "He 's used to it, I s'pose."

They took him to Dale's house, and found the family in bed. Mr. Dale had been to the house-raising, but returned before the boys did.

The family were aroused, and made acquainted with the affair, and a rousing fire was built, before which he was laid.

"I 'm afraid he 's badly frozen," said Dale. The man was insensible.

"So am I," replied Abraham; "and I will stay and help you take care of him through the night."

"I think you better. By the looks of him, I shall want somebody to help."

"Then I'll stay, boys," continued Abraham, "if you'll go round on your way back and let mother know where I am. Tell her I'll be along early in the morning."

The boys agreed to do this, and left, conversing on their way about the affair, and remarking upon the kindness and generosity of Abraham. The merciful offer of the latter to stay and take care of the man was only a fair, illustration of his general good feelings. His benevolent heart felt for the needy and suffering. It was unusual for a youth to exhibit so much true tenderness for the unfortunate and distressed as he did. The neighbors observed it, and commented upon it. This was one of the traits of character that made him a favorite with all who knew him. He was unselfish, disinterested, and self-sacrificing. He would cheerfully forego a night's rest to help the intemperate man. He thought more of the drunkard's safety than he did of his own ease. And there are many of his personal acquaintances in our land who will bear witness that, from that day to this, this amiable quality of heart has won him admiring friends.

We need say no more of this affair, than that Myers rallied from his insensibility during the night, and early the next morning he started homeward. Abraham was satisfied with the night's labor.

We must not omit to mention that about this time Abraham's sister was married to a young man in the neighborhood, and one year after the nuptials were celebrated she died, rolling another great wave of sorrow over her brother's heart.

There remains but one other event of his life in Indiana that we shall narrate, and this occurred just after the heavy loss experienced by the death of his sister. It relates to that brief portion of his life that was devoted to flat-boating.

XVII.

TRIP TO NEW ORLEANS.

"WHAT say you, Abe, about takin' a flat-boat to New Orleans for me ?" inquired a man whom we shall call Peters, as he met Abraham when he was on the way to see his father upon the subject.

"I don't know," answered Abraham, rather at a loss to know whether his interrogator was in earnest or not.

"I 'm not joking, Abe ; I have a quantity of stores that I am going to forward to New Orleans, and I thought you and John might take a flat-boat there. What say you to a bargain ?"

"I should like to go, if we can do it," answered Abraham. "Is John used to the business ?" John was Mr. Peters's eldest son.

"About the same that you are. But I thought that both of you together might manage to make the trip."

The fact was, that Mr. Peters had entire confidence in Abraham's tact at doing things, as well as in his fidelity, so that he would feel safer to give up the management of the boat to him rather than to his son. As he always did everything well, Mr. Peters expected that he would do this well, — a very good premise from which to derive such a conclusion.

"I am ready to undertake it, if father is willing," continued Abraham. "Perhaps he will be afraid to have me go."

"I rather think not. I will see him, if you are disposed to go."

"Well, I am disposed to go."

"And it will suit John fust-rate to have you go.'

"How long before you will want to have us start?"

"Just as soon as I can get ready; I should say, within two weeks."

"I can go then as well as any time," said Abraham.

"I 'm going to see your father now."

Mr. Peters proceeded to have an interview with Mr. Lincoln, and Abraham went with him.

"How long will they be gone?" inquired Mr. Lincoln.

"That depends on circumstances."

"Rather venturesome for such young fellers," said Mr. Lincoln.

"And many hardships, too," remarked his mother.

"And not a little pleasure, I expect," responded Abraham, looking as if he coveted the berth.

"Flat-boatmen see hard times," continued Mr. Lincoln.

"And so have you seen hard times," answered Mr. Peters. "And as to that matter, all of us have seen some hard times, I reckon."

"Of course, and I don't expect my boy will steer clear of all these things; but this is new business for him."

"Yes, and none the worse for that."

"He may not do so well for you; that is what I was thinkin' of."

"As to that, Abe does everything well, and that is the reason I want to hire him. I will pay him well for it."

"How much?"

"Ten dollars a month; and that is a good price for a boy of his age."

"He is wuth just as much to you for that business as an older man with no more experience. He is strong, and able to endure as much as any one."

"That may be, and that is why I am earnest to have him go; and I know, too, that I can trust him. There is considerable to look after in such an enterprise."

"Almost too much for two such boys to have."

"Not with Abe to oversee and manage," said Mr. Peters.

"Well, I am not afraid to risk him, if you ain't," added Mr. Lincoln. "I know he will do as well as he can."

"And that's as well as I want he should do. So I understand that the bargain is made?"

"Yes, if you say so."

"You had my 'say so' some time ago. Be on hand, Abe." The last remark was addressed to Abraham, as Mr. Peters turned to leave.

Abraham was delighted with the prospect before him. Such a trip, on such business, suited him exactly. We will not stop to follow him through the interim of two weeks; but while he is getting ready, we will give some account of flat-boating on the Western waters.

For some years there had been a class of boatmen, fearless, hardy, athletic men, who "traversed the longest rivers, penetrated the most remote wilderness upon their watery routes, and kept up a trade and intercourse between the most distant points."

They were exposed to great perils, and were out shelterless in all kinds of weather. With no bed but the deck of their boats on which to lie at night, and no covering but a blanket, they spent months and years of their existence.

It was on such boats that the rich cargoes ascending the Mississippi were carried. By human labor, they were propelled against the strong current for nearly two thousand miles; and it was a labor that required great muscular strength, and remarkable powers of endurance. The result was that a class of men were trained in this business of unusual courage, and proud only of their ability to breast storms and endure hardships.

In addition to this class, whose life-business it was to propel these Western boats, there were those who occasionally made a trip to New Orleans to sell their stores. Sometimes several farmers, or other persons, would club together and make out a cargo, and send it down to New Orleans; and sometimes one alone would do the same. This was the case with Mr. Peters. He had a quantity of stores suited to meet the wants of the sugar plantations in Louisiana, and he wanted to convert them into cash. Money was very scarce, and many families, like that of Mr. Lincoln, saw but little. What was in circulation was brought into the Western country by people moving thither from the East, or was obtained, as Mr. Peters proposed to obtain some, by sending a boat-load of stores to New Orleans.

At that time the merchants did not trade in corn, flour, pork, wheat, beef, &c., as they do now. They bought beeswax, feathers, and tallow, and traded in furs and peltries. They did not send the products of the country to the East to liquidate their debts, for satisfactory exchanges could then be made through the United States Bank. But now that order of things has entirely changed, and the flat-boat is no longer used in commerce.

But Abraham had agreed to become a flat-boatman, at least for a time, and the day of his departure was at hand

"Eighteen hundred miles is rather of a long trip for a feller who has n't seen more of the world than you have, Abe," said his father.

"None too long," replied Abraham. "I shall see some of the world now, if I never have before."

"And perhaps see the bottom of the Mississippi, too."

"I am not afraid of that."

"But hundreds have lost their lives in this way, and men who have been used to the business, too."

"That is no sign that I shall."

"It is no sign you won't," answered his father. "It 's well enough to think on 't."

"But I sha'n't borrow any trouble about it."

"I don't ask you to do that; but it 's wuth while to think that you may be sent into eternity by some accident."

"If you don't want I should go, I will give it up now." Abraham inferred from his father's tone and manner of speaking, that he had given his consent against his better judgment, and he was bound not to go against his father's will.

"I *do* want you should go. I was only tellin' some of my thoughts. I can't help thinkin'."

"It may be the best thing for me that I ever did."

"Yes; if no accident happens to you, I have no doubt that it will be a real good school for you.

But it is a long ways to go, and a long time for you to be gone."

"But I have got to go some time, and I may as well begin now."

"I know it; but that makes it no easier for me to have you go. However, it don't do no good to talk about it now. I have said you might go, and you may, and I want you should go."

So Abraham and his associate, John, embarked upon their flat-boat at the appointed time, bound for New Orleans. Their cargo was destined for a sugar plantation, and they had received all necessary instructions, and bade their friends "good by." It was a beautiful day, and the Ohio never appeared more charming to young adventurers. Their voyage began auspiciously, and their young hearts were full of glee.

"I say, Abe, how many times you goin' to upset before reachin' the Mississippi?" asked John.

"I hardly think we shall do it more than once," answered Abraham, "unless you have a better faculty than I have to load up again in the water."

"I did n't think of that; it would be a hard matter to reload at the bottom of the river."

"Yes; and we must look out for accidents, or your father will wish he had never sent us. I hope we shall make a capital thing of it."

"I hope so, too, or we shall never have another such a chance. The old man never would have sent me if it had n't been for you, Abe."

"How so?"

"Because he thinks you can do most anything that's possible, and so he was willing to risk me and all the cargo with you."

"Pshaw! You are fooling now."

"No such thing; it's the living truth. I expect he thought that you could keep me and the cargo from sinkin', if we did upset."

"Well, my father rather expects the opposite, I judge by his talk," replied Abraham. "He thinks it is rather of a risky piece of business to send us on such a trip."

"Why did he let you go?"

"I hardly know; I thought, after he had promised to let me go, that he was going to alter his mind."

"You would n't liked that."

"Not I, though I should have stayed at home if he had said so."

"Should?"

"Of course; it would be too bad to go against his will."

"Not if you made a good thing of it."

"That would n't make it right."

It must answer our purpose to say simply, that they continued the voyage with as much courage and hope as they began it. At night they tied up their boat close to the bank of the river, in some favorable spot, and lay down upon their "running board," as a flat-boat was sometimes called, for sleep. They had no bed, — nothing but the hard deck, with a blanket to cover them. True, this was not so great a change for boys who were reared in the wilderness, living in a house without a floor, or a feather-bed, or a pane of glass, as it would be for boys of this day who are used to the comforts and conveniences of affluent homes. Still it was a change, and many of their nights were extremely lonely.

Their voyage was not monotonous. The scenery was continually changing, and they frequently passed other boats with their merry crews, and held conversations with people who flocked to the banks of the river from adjacent villages. "Where are you from?" "Where are you bound?" "What are you loaded with?" were questions that they frequently had to answer.

The days were not all sunshine. Heavy storms sometimes descended upon them, and they had to exert themselves to the utmost to keep their little craft right side up. Day after day they were drenched with rain, and still they must keep on the voyage. Violent storms sometimes raged at night, the wind blowing almost a hurricane, and the rain pouring down in torrents, and still there was no alternative, — they must make their bed on their little boat and take the pelting of the storm. These were times that tried their spirit, and yet they had no complaints to utter. Never for a moment did Abraham wish he had not undertaken the voyage. He was not accustomed to undertake a work, and fail to accomplish it. He always finished what he began, and started with that determination.

They were approaching their place of destination. As their cargo was designed for the sugar plantations, they drew up to the sugar coast on the north of the city of New Orleans to trade. They took measures to advertise their wares, and found ready customers. On the night after their arrival an incident occurred that we will narrate. They had fastened their boat, and, much wearied with the labors of the day, they laid down at an early hour to rest. About midnight Abraham was startled by a noise.

"What 's that?" he whispered to his companion, who was still asleep.

Instead of a reply from John, he distinctly heard low voices within a few feet from the boat, as if trouble was brewing.

"John! John!" he whispered, shaking him at the same time. And while John was waking out of a sound sleep, Abraham was straining his eyes to see what he could discover through the darkness. He was satisfied that he could discern the figures of several men on the bank of the river.

"John! there 's trouble for us."

"What is it?" Both spoke in a whisper.

"Foul play, I think. Hark!" Both listened, and the low muttering of voices could be heard.

"Niggers," whispered John. "They don't mean anything."

"They would n't be here at this time of night, if they did n't. They know we 've been trading and taking money."

"There! I see the figures of a number moving this way," said John. "I guess there is trouble for us."

"I know there is," answered Abraham; "and we must defend ourselves to the last. *Who 's there?*" And he shouted this inquiry with much emphasis, at the same time seizing a billet of wood that lay near him.

"WHO 'S THERE?" he shouted again.

"Dar ole nigger," was the response from one of the negroes; for it turned out that there were seven slaves.

"What are you here for? Off with yourselves," replied Abraham. But the words had scarcely dropped from his lips, when one of the number leaped upon the boat by one dexterous bound. But no sooner did he strike the boat than Abraham knocked him into the water with his billet.

"We must fight, John; they mean to murder us. Strike for your life!" By this time John was armed with a cudgel and nerved for the struggle.

And he soon had an opportunity to fight; for no sooner was the first intruder knocked into the water than four others bounded upon the boat. Heavy blows were dealt upon them, until it became a hand-to-hand fight, so that billets could not be used.

"Knock them into the water, Abe," shouted John; and that was just what Abraham was trying to do.

After a severe struggle, lasting some ten minutes, they succeeded in tumbling three of the number into the water, whereupon the fourth made his escape.

"Come, John, let 's after them on the shore," cried Abraham. And no sooner said than done. Before the last three who were plunged into the water had crawled up the bank, Abraham was pounding two of them on the shore with his club. The first one whom he knocked into the water had reached the bank, and he fled from his antagonist as he would have done from a tiger. And by the time the other three crawled out of their cold bath, the two boys had driven the four on shore away at the top of their speed.

"Here, John, give it to these," exclaimed Abraham.

And they pounced upon the three crawling out of the water, dealing heavy blows upon them before they had time to rally upon the bank. The negroes were thoroughly terrified at their unexpected reception. They had not counted upon the strength and courage of the two young boatmen. They supposed it would be an easy matter for seven of them to make way with two youth like them, and then rob the boat. But the young men saw that it was a case of life and death, and they fought with desperation. They had no doubt that the negroes meant to murder them, and then rob them and the boat, and they fought accordingly. Abraham's strength was almost superhuman on the occasion, and the negroes were badly bruised and maimed by his blows. They were armed with clubs, and they laid them upon Abraham and John so as to injure them considerably. But the latter came out of the battle victorious. The negroes escaped as best they could.

"Are you hurt much, John?" inquired Abraham.

"No great; got a few hard knocks. How is it with you?"

"Lamed my arm; one of 'em hit me a cut across my right eye, too. But I have no fault to find, since we saved our necks."

"We must get the boat off now as quick as possible," said John, "or they 'll be back with twice their number."

"I thought of that; you jump aboard, and I will untie the boat. We must lose no time, neither."

In a minute John was aboard, and scarcely another minute had passed before Abraham followed him, having loosed the boat.

"We are safe now, if the whole plantation comes," said John, as they shoved off into the stream.

"We sha'n't need to go far," added Abraham. "Only change our position, and we are safe."

"That may be, but I think I shall sleep with my eyes open the rest of the night."

"And I will keep you company," responded Abraham. "The next time I come to New Orleans, I shall come armed. This going to war without a gun is not quite the thing."

"I wish we had been armed," said John. "Would n't we made the feathers fly?"

"The *wool*, you mean," replied Abraham, jocosely. He had become as cool as if nothing had happened.

"They meant to kill us."

"Of course they did. It would n't have done for them to rob us, and leave us to tell the story to their master. But they might have made way with us, and robbed and sunk the boat, and nobody been any the wiser for it."

"They are no fools, if they be niggers."

"No; but after all they are not so much to blame as their masters," added Abraham. "Slavery has robbed *them* of everything, and so I s'pose they think it is fair play to take what they can get."

They succeeded in selling their cargo well, and returned in safety to Indiana. The venturesome enterprise for two such youth turned out a capital thing, and when their narrow escape was known, the trip on the flat-boat was talked of as a wonderful expedition, and Abraham received the credit of being a good boatman, manager, salesman, as well as a courageous defender of number one. The success was ascribed to his tact, judgment, fidelity, and force of character.

XVIII.

REMOVAL TO ILLINOIS.

SOON after Abraham's trip to New Orleans, the most glowing accounts of the fertility of the prairie lands of Illinois began to spread in the older States. They reached the Lincoln family early, and the father began to talk of moving. From month to month the news from Illinois concerning the richness and productiveness of the soil grew more and more interesting, and a tide of emigration at once set towards that State. Mr. Lincoln became desirous of moving thither himself, and Abraham was earnest to go. Accordingly, for the purpose of ascertaining the exact truth of the matter, and selecting a good location to settle, Dennis Hanks, a relative of Abraham's step-mother, was delegated to proceed to Illinois on a tour of investigation. Lincoln did not wish to move without knowing more of the country than he could gather from rumor.

It was two years after the aforesaid news from Illinois reached the Lincoln family before they were ready to move. The journey of Hanks thither fully confirmed all they had heard, and this decided the matter of their removal. It was not, however, until March, 1830, that they were prepared to start.

There were three families to move, and twelve persons in all, — the family of Mr. Lincoln, and the families of his wife's two daughters, who came to Indiana, and settled near her.

Abraham was just twenty-one years old, and therefore free. But he was still a faithful son.

"You are your own man now," said his father.

"What of that?" was Abraham's reply, suspecting what thoughts were in his mind.

"Why, you can go or stay, though I don't see how I can get along without you."

"Nor I; and I want to go to Illinois more than you do, and I shall see you safely there, and settled down, before I leave you."

"I'm glad of that," continued his father. "I won't ask you to stay at home one minute after we get settled down. You ought to be lookin' out for yourself, now you are of age."

"We 'll talk about that when we get there. Perhaps I shall find enough to do for a while to get you fixed up, and I can attend to that better than you can."

"Well, it's a long ways there, and I'm almost sorry that I undertook it at my time of life. It looks like a great job to get there, and begin new."

"It don't to me. We 'll be there, and have a roof over our heads, in less than four weeks."

"If nothin' happens, you mean."

"There will something happen, I'm thinking," answered Abraham, dryly, "or we shall never get there."

"What?"

"I expect that it will happen that we shall go there in about two weeks, by hard travelling. If that don't happen, I shall be sorry."

"We shall see," added Mr. Lincoln.

The fact was, Abraham thought too much of his father and mother to leave them to undertake such a journey alone. No money could have hired him to leave them before they were settled in Illinois. Mr. Scripps, who knows all the circumstances well, says, "He was the only son of his father, now advanced in years; and it was not in his nature to desert his aged sire at a time when all the hardships, privations, and toil of making a new home in a new country were about to be entered upon. Whatever the future may have seemed to hold in it, as a reward for effort specially directed to that end, he cheerfully put aside in obedience to his sense of duty, and engaged at once and heartily in the work before him."

A son of so much consideration and fidelity will not fail to make his mark.

The above writer, a Western man himself, describes the manner of moving in those days, as follows: —

"In those days, when people changed their residence from one State or settlement to another, they took all their movable possessions with them,—their household goods, their kitchen utensils, including provisions for the journey, their farming implements, their horses and cattle. The former were loaded into wagons, drawn, for the most part, by oxen; and the latter were driven by the smaller boys of the family, who were sometimes assisted by their sisters and mother. Thus arranged for a journey of weeks,—not unfrequently of months,—the emigrant set out, thinking but little of the hardships before him,—of bad roads, of unbridged streams, of disagreeable weather, of sleeping on the ground or in the wagon, of sickness, accidents, and sometimes death by the way,—dwelling chiefly in thought upon the novelty and excitement of the trip, the rumored attractions of the new country whither he was going, and of the probable advantages likely to result from the change. By ten or fifteen miles per day, over untravelled roads, now across mountains, swamps, and watercourses, and now through dense, umbrageous forests, and across broad prairies where the horizon alone bounded the vision, the caravan of wagons, men, women, and children, flocks and herds, toiled onward by day, sleeping under the broad canopy of stars at night, patiently accomplishing the destined journey, sometimes of weeks', some times of months' duration."

In this manner the Lincoln family moved. They had two ox-teams to carry the goods of the three families, — one team of two oxen, and the other of four. Abraham drove the latter. The journey which they proposed to undertake was almost two hundred miles; yet, for the perseverance and heroism of pioneer families, it was not a very great undertaking.

The weather proved favorable nearly all the way, though the roads were excessively muddy. For miles, Abraham walked through mud a foot deep. Often, for a long distance, he waded in water up to his knees (and it is well known that his knees were not very low down). When they had performed nearly one hundred and fifty miles of the journey, they came to the Kaskaskia River, where they found the bottom lands overflowed, and the old corduroy road nearly gone.

"We 're done to now," said Hanks.

"I don't know about that," answered Abraham. "Let us see about it."

"It is plain enough to see, I should think. The man who directed us back there yesterday said, if the bottom was overflowed, it would be three miles through water, and I should think it was more than that."

"I don't care if it 's twice three," replied Abraham; "if it 's not too deep to wade."

"We can wait some days for the water to fall, or

we can go up or down the river a few miles, and possibly find a better place to cross," suggested Hanks.

"That will take too much time. The water won't fall yet a while. It is only the middle of March, you know, and the rivers are always high. I am for going straight ahead through thick and thin."

"That's the only way, I think," said Mr. Lincoln, who had listened to the conversation, while he was looking rather doubtfully upon the flood of water before them."

"We can't stay here for the water to fall, that's certain," continued Abraham, "and as to finding a better place to cross, I don't believe we can, if we go around twenty miles."

"And that would take time, too," suggested his father.

"Yes, and I am for going right along. I will go forward; and if I go under, the rest of you may take warning." This remark was made rather in a strain of pleasantry, to inspire all hearts around him with courage. "Come, Dennis, what do you say? Will you follow me?"

"Of course; I can go where you can."

It was settled to go forward, turning neither to the right hand nor left. And for three miles Abraham drove his team through water that was up to his waist, urging his oxen along, and cheering the hearts of the company with words of encouragement. His usual energy and force of character enabled him to overcome this difficulty, as the same elements of success have served him well many times from that day to this.

They accomplished the journey from Spencer County, Indiana, to Decatur, Illinois, in fifteen days. The spot selected for their home was on the north side of the Sangamon River, about ten miles west of Decatur, — a spot wisely chosen, because it was at the junction of the timber and prairie lands.

A log-house was immediately erected, in the building of which Abraham acted a conspicuous part. Ten acres of prairie land was selected, and the sods broken for a crop of corn.

"That must be fenced at once," said Abraham.

"And you 'll have to split the rails, if it is done," replied his father.

"That I can do, as I am used to it; but I don't expect to split rails for a living all my days."

"I hope you won't have to. When we get things under way, you can seek your fortin' somewhere else."

"I have n't made up my mind as to that. There will be time enough for that when the ten acres are fenced in."

"We shall have enough to do this summer to break up and plant ten acres of corn, and take care of it, and fence the lot. But who ever saw such land as this? The half was not told us?" Mr. Lincoln was surprised at the richness of the lands; and, in all respects, he was pleased with the change of residence.

"There can be no better farming land than this," answered Abraham; "and it ain't half the work to cultivate these prairie lands. And I am just the hand to fence them, as I have swung the axe so much."

"Yes, you can do it better than I can, and a great deal quicker; so you may go at it as soon as you please."

Accordingly, Abraham proceeded to split the rails for the ten-acre lot. These are the rails about which so much was said in the late Presidential campaign. "Their existence," says Mr. Scripps, "was brought to the public attention during the sitting of the Republican State Convention, at Decatur, on which occasion a banner, attached to two of these rails, and bearing an appropriate inscription, was brought into the assemblage and formally presented to that body, amid a scene of unparalleled enthusiasm. After that, they were in demand in every State of the Union in which free labor is honored, where they were borne in processions of the people, and hailed by hundreds of thousands of freemen as a symbol of triumph, and as a glorious vindication of freedom, and of the rights and the dignity of free labor. These, however, were far from being the first or only rails made by Lincoln. He was a practised hand at the business. His first lessons had been taken while yet a boy in Indiana. Some of the rails made by him in that State have been clearly identified. The writer has seen a cane, now in the possession of Mr. Lincoln, made by one of his old Indiana acquaintances, from one of those rails split by his own hands in boyhood."

Thus was he reared to labor. He believed in labor. He was not ashamed to labor. Louis Philippe said, when he occupied the throne of France, that he himself was the only monarch of Europe who was qualified for his place, for the reason that he was the only one who could black his own boots. If self-help is a necessary qualification for a ruler, then Abraham was always qualifying himself to rule.

That summer of hard toil passed, and the golden harvests of autumn repaid the laborer for his sweat and fatigue ; and Abraham was still at home. Winter set in early, and proved to be the severest one ever known in all that region. That was the winter of the "great snow," as it was called, when for weeks it was three feet deep upon a level. In consequence there was much suffering. It was a trying winter for cattle. Beasts suffered as well as men. The Lincoln family were well supplied with corn, but their supply of meat was scanty. As their dependence for animal food was mainly upon the rifle, the deep snow interfered very much with their supply. But for Abraham's capacity to endure, the family would have suffered. He could brave any degree of cold, and experience almost any hardship, and not be overcome. Consequently, he wallowed through the snow to shoot deer and other wild animals for food; and he was successful in providing food for the family. He was not a noted hunter. Although he began to use the rifle in boyhood with a good deal of enthusiasm, yet his love of books was so much stronger than his love of this sport, that he seldom went hunting except when it was absolutely necessary to obtain food for the family. One of his early associates writes upon this subject: "We seldom went hunting together. Abe was not a noted hunter, as the time spent by other boys in such amusements was improved by him in the perusal of some good book."

During that memorable winter, however, he behaved like a veteran hunter, and kept the bear of hunger at bay. The family realized that they owed much to his devotion and remarkable powers of endurance.

XIX.

NEW FRIENDS.

"I S'POSE you must go," said Mr. Lincoln, "and I know it is best." Abraham was about leaving home to seek his fortune. It was just as the spring opened, after the severe winter named in the last chapter.

"If I am ever going, it is high time now. But I could n't go till I saw you comfortably fixed here."

"Well, we are comfortable now, and you won't see a better time for it than this."

"I think so."

"And you are in a good part of the country to make a trial."

"Much better than Indiana would be."

"And better still than Kentucky," added his father.

"I could n't live in a Slave State anyhow." He had become thoroughly imbued with his father's views and feelings in regard to slavery; and his own generous and humane nature was sufficient in itself to make him a foe to the wicked system.

"I shall have your clothes ready by to-morrow,"

said his mother, who sat plying the needle with all her might, "though I'd much rather you would wear 'em up at home."

"Perhaps I should rather wear them up here," replied Abraham. "It won't be any easier for me to live anywhere else."

"I am glad you think so." And this was said with a good deal of feeling by his step-mother; for she had learned to look upon him with about the same maternal feeling that she did upon her own children.

Abraham left home. He had no particular plans about the future. He felt, however, that there was something in the world for him to do, and he would do it. So he went forth, rather late in life to begin for himself, but possessing principles and elements of character that were more valuable to him than thousands of gold and silver.

As we have said, it was just as the spring opened after the winter of the "great snow." He went into the vicinity of Petersburg, Menard County, and labored where he could find work. During that summer and fall, he worked some for a man by the name of Armstrong, — a poor man, somewhat advanced in life. Said Armstrong had but one child living, — a son about fourteen years of age at that time, uncultivated, and not always obedient. His parents had indulged him to his injury, and they were still blind to their folly.

Abraham was so intelligent, accommodating, upright, and faithful, that he won the hearts of the aged couple. They possessed three or four old volumes of books, and he read them through and through. He borrowed others, too, and read them in his leisure hours. He studied his old arithmetic a little, also, and altogether was rather student-like in his habits. He was certainly a striking contrast with their boy.

"I don't understand it," said Armstrong to his wife.

"Don't understand what?"

"Why, how Abe, who was brought up in the backwoods as I was, should take to books so."

The reader will observe that his old nickname stuck to him, though he had left home.

"I 've thought of it over and over. He talks like a schoolmaster."

"There ain't half the schoolmasters who can talk as well as he can. They don't know half so much. Then he can be trusted with anything."

"Anybody can see that; and I guess the Bible is at the bottom of it."

"It would n't be strange. I never saw a feller who can repeat more of the Bible than he can; and he respects it, too."

"He had a good mother, too. I 've talked with him about it, and she must have been a smart woman."

"He 's seen hard times, too. According to his story, he and his father both have fared worse than we have."

"Yes; and I think it is a fine thing that he come about here to live."

"That 's what I think; and I 'll tell you what I 've concluded on, if you are willin'."

"What is it?"

"Well, it may be that he won't have work in the winter, and I 've been thinkin' that it would be servin' him a good turn to let him stay here, and make it his home with us. He 's a real scholar, and likes a book better than anything, though he works better than any man that I ever hired, and will do more work in a day."

"I shall agree to that," answered Mrs. Armstrong. "There 's no tellin' how much good he may do our boy. Then he may be of some use to us, if it 's a hard winter."

"He won't allers work round so," continued Mr. Armstrong. "He knows too much for that. Remember what I tell you, — that boy won't allers dig away at this rate."

The proposition was made to Abraham, and he accepted it, with the condition that he would render service to the family sufficient to pay for his board. They consented to let the matter stand so, though they still intended to do him a favor.

We might say here, that there was the evidence

of rigid honesty and the desire to do right in Abraham's daily demeanor, no matter what he was about. Wherever he went, people were soon impressed with his high-toned principles. He was a marked young man. There was that in his appearance that attracted attention at once.

All this was manifest during that season of his residence near Petersburg. The young people who became acquainted with him gave him their confidence without hesitation. They believed him to be a conscientious, upright young man. For this reason, they referred the settlement of disputes to him. They had confidence in his judgment, as well as his honesty. Different sorts of games were in vogue at that time, and running-matches and horse-racings, and if Abraham was present, one party or the other was sure to make him their "judge." Two years later, while he was living in New Salem, he shared the confidence of all to such an extent that *both* parties, in the aforesaid amusements, were wont to choose him for their "judge." In all cases, too, there was the utmost satisfaction shown in his decisions.

It was at this period of his life that he was christened "HONEST ABE." It was so unusual for the same person to act as "judge" for both of the contending parties, and it was expressive of so much confidence in his character, that by common consent he came to be known as "HONEST ABE."

" A good book was preferable to a good suit of clothes." — Page 227.

He found himself with his new friends in their log-cabin when winter set in. There he sits with his book, studying by the light of the fire through the long winter evenings, while the aged couple occupy their wonted seats, the old man huddling over the fire as usual, and his industrious partner looking the very picture of cheerfulness. Abraham's dress is rather worse for the wear, — a matter about which he did not particularly concern himself. A good book was preferable to a good suit of clothes, in his view, and for this reason he was content with his lot.

During the winter he added several volumes to his stock of books by purchase, though his principal object was to pursue his arithmetic. Hitherto he had accomplished little more than to retain the knowledge of the science that he acquired at the school of Mr. Crawford. He desired to pursue the study, and master the whole book, — a task that he successfully performed.

The spring was at hand, when one day Mr. Armstrong returned from a trip to a neighboring town with good tidings for Abraham.

"I 've seen a man," he said, "who wants to hire two or three hands to help him take a flat-boat to New Orleans; and I told him that you would make a capital hand, Abe. What do you say to it?"

"I 'm ready for it, if he 's the right sort of a man," answered Abraham.

"Well, he is. It is Denton Offutt, who trades so much up and down the river. I think he has a store and mill at New Salem."

"When does he want help?"

"Just as soon as the snow is off. He is going to buy a boat at Beardstown." This was the port of departure for New Orleans.

"I should rather like the business," continued Abraham. "I know something about it, too. How much will he pay a month?"

"A good price, I reckon, by what he said; and he thought you was just the man for him, after I told him about you."

"Will he come here to see me?" Abraham would not lose the opportunity, so that he was solicitous lest the chance might slip.

"Yes; he 's coming this way on business in a few days, and he 'll give us a call."

"There is no doubt about it, is there?"

"No, I don't think there is; that is what he said, anyhow."

"If I thought he would n't come, I would go to see him at once. I should like the chance, and I don't want to lose it."

"He 'll come, I 've no doubt, after all I told him about you. He 's a fool, if he don't."

"Perhaps he won't think so," said Abraham, rather amused at the last remark of his aged friend.

Mr. Offutt was good as his word, and he hired

Abraham for fifteen dollars a month, — rather extra pay for that time. But he saw at a glance that he was just the young man he wanted.

It was arranged that Abraham and the other young men whom Offutt hired should meet him at Springfield at the time appointed, from whence they would proceed to Beardstown.

Accordingly, Abraham made ready for his new business, bade his kind friends, the Armstrongs, good-by, and started off. It was with a truly grateful heart that he left the hospitable roof that had afforded him friendly shelter, and he went forth resolved that the kind-hearted couple should not be losers on his account.

On reaching Springfield, he found that Offutt could not purchase a boat, as he expected, and hence a boat must be built for the purpose. As Abraham could turn his hand to almost anything, Offutt proposed that he should proceed to Sangamon, on the Sangamon River, in company with the other young men hired, and there build a boat. Sangamon was near where the Chicago, Alton, and St. Louis Railroad now crosses the Sangamon River. This proposition was accepted, and the boat was built.

The trip to New Orleans was made, and it was very successful. Offutt was impressed with the superior abilities of Abraham. Mr. Scripps says, "He [Abraham] bore himself so well throughout, — was so faithful in all the trusts reposed in him by his employer, — so active, prompt, and efficient in all necessary labor, — so cool, determined, and full of resources in the presence of danger, — that before reaching New Orleans Offutt had become greatly attached to him, and on their return engaged him to take the general charge of his store and mill in the village of New Salem."

Hence Abraham came on the flat-boat to New Salem, where he was installed over the mercantile interests of the place. How well he succeeded will appear in the pages that follow.

XX.

A MERCHANT'S CLERK.

ABRAHAM soon became the most important man in the place; for in those days the merchant was second to no man in the community. In this case, also, there was an additional reason for his popularity. For he was one of those social, affable, intelligent young men who make friends wherever they go; and, on this account, he drew around himself a circle of ardent friends, who looked upon him as the pride of the village.

"The best fellow we 've had in the store yet," said William Greene, an intelligent young man, to a number of his companions; "he knows a thing or two."

"I 'll bet you that is so," replied Nelson Day; "it is real fun to hear him talk."

"And he is so accommodating and straightforward! Mother says she 'd trust him with anything, because he 's so honest. She paid him a few cents too much the other day, and he told her of it, and gave it back to her."

"Not many on 'em who 'd do that," said Nelson.

"Everybody says that he gives Scripture weight and measure."

"And he is none of your high-fly gentry," added William, "if he does keep store. He knows more in a half an hour than Offutt's other man did in a week."

"Yes, and he 's drawing customers that have n't traded there before, just because he does the thing that is right. Everybody knows that he won't lie nor cheat; and they believe just what he says, and they like to trade with him on that account."

"Offutt was a fortunate man to get him to keep his store," continued William. "It will be money in his pocket."

"And he seems to attend to the business just as closely as he would if it was his own," said Nelson; "he is there early and late, and he is allers readin' when he has nothin' else to do."

"That 's because he is honest," replied William; "a dishonest clerk would n't care whether the business prospered or not, nor whether people were pleased or not. Offutt is off so much that he would n't know whether a clerk was faithful or not, and its lucky for him that he hit upon Abe as he did."

"And it 's about as lucky for us. I tell you how 't is: that store is now just about the best place to go to that there is anywhere about. Abe is the greatest feller on stories that I ever heard, and many of them are real facts of history. You ought to hear him tell about Washington and Franklin, as he did the other day. He knows a heap more about them than old 'Squire Jones ; and he 'll talk politics like a member of Congress."

"And he can't be beat, nuther," said a third companion. "How he did use up Stokes and Parkhurst, the other day, who think they are great on arguing! He showed 'em that they did n't know what they were talkin' about."

"How did Stokes bear it?" inquired William. "He is a rabid fellow, and it would be just like him to blaze away with madness."

"He did n't; Abe was so pleasant and funny about it, and topped off with one of his best stories, so that Stokes shook his sides with laughter."

"And I heard him say, no longer ago than yesterday," said Nelson, "that Abe was a plaguy smart feller! He likes him first-rate."

"I can see through it," replied William. "Abe is so much of a gentleman, and keeps so cool himself, and mixes in his stories so nicely, that no decent man can get mad. But as Stokes is hardly decent, I did n't know but he might flare up, and have one of his tantrums."

"Well, he did n't, and you must give him the credit of it."

"I will do that, you may be sure."

"Nor forget to credit Abe with the way he has of doing things," added another.

Thus Abraham won the young people of New Salem, at the same time that he pleased their fathers and mothers. He was the centre of attraction to the young people of the place, and they really felt honored to make his acquaintance. They looked up to him as to a superior, and sought his advice on various projects that young people are disposed to start. "Abe's say so" was the upshot of the matter, and it settled the question, whatever it might be. Never did a young person of his age have more influence over associates than he, and the secret of it is clear. First, they had confidence in him, on account of his honesty; second, they were in love with his knowledge, acquired by the careful improvement of his leisure time; third, his gentlemanly bearing and courtesy impressed them favorably.

As to the confidence and respect that his honesty won, too much cannot be said of it. His case furnishes a vindication of the following sentiments from the Merchant's Magazine: —

"Integrity of character and truth are the prerequisites for success in any calling, and especially so in that of the merchant. These are attributes of the man which never fail to command respect and win admiration. There is no better stock in trade than these commodities; no capital goes so far, or pays so well, or is so exempt from bankruptcy and loss. When known, it gives credit and confidence, and in the hardest of times will honor your paper in bank. It gives you an unlimited capital to do business on, and everybody will indorse your paper, and the general faith of mankind will be your guaranty that you will not fail. Let every young man in commencing business look well to these indispensable elements of success, and guard and defend them as he would the apple of his eye. If inattentive and reckless here, he will imperil everything. Bankruptcy in character is seldom repaired in an ordinary lifetime. A man may suffer in reputation, and recover, — not so the man who suffers in character. Be just and truthful. Let these be the ruling and predominating principles of your life, and the rewards will be certain, either in the happiness they bring to your own bosom, or the success which will attend upon all your business operations in life, — or both."

To return. Abraham had been engaged in this new business about three months, when Nelson Day called at the store to see him, as he frequently did, and found him alone.

"Readin', as usual!" he exclaimed; for he found his new and valued friend poring over a book.

"No, not exactly reading," replied Abraham. "This is a grammar that I have."

"Studyin' grammar, then?"

"Yes; I want to know something about it. I never did."

"Nor I, and that ain't the worst on 't"; and Nelson laughed as he said it.

"Well, I intend to know a little of it," added Abraham. "It is rather dry, but I am determined to master it, if I can. I want, at least, to discover whether I am a common noun or not."

"You 're an *uncommon* noun, Abe," said Nelson, meaning to compliment his friend, at the same time that he got off a pun.

"Your word for it."

"Of course, my word for it. But I am quite sure that if there is anything in that book, you will get it out."

"But really, Nelson, this is a very important study, and I think that every one ought to understand it, if they can."

"Not many know anything about it," answered Nelson.

"And that does not prove that it is useless. There are a great many things of importance that many people know nothing about."

"That 's so; but most people have got along without it. My father and mother never studied it in their lives, and I never did, and we 've got along well enough so far without it."

"Perhaps you would have got along better with it. I 've learned enough already to be of great service to me, and I intend to know more yet."

" But there 's a customer, and you won't learn much more now," added Nelson: "down with your book."

The customer was promptly served, and the conversation with Nelson suspended until the buyer left the store.

" It would be a hard case for me," said Nelson, when the customer was gone, " to learn anything in such a place."

" You would get used to it," replied Abraham, " and 'Practice makes perfect,' you know. Some days I have two or three hours of leisure time."

" But it is only a little at a time. You just get at it, and somebody comes. I don't think much of that."

" We don't all think alike."

" That 's a fact; I 'm pretty sure that if you thought as I do, you would n't be troublin' your brains over that grammar."

" Perhaps nobody else would, and the 'king's English' would be shockingly murdered. We should have another Babel almost."

" How is that? For the life of me, I can't see any particular good that comes of studyin' grammar."

" That is because you have not even looked at the definition of it. Grammar is the art of speaking and writing the English language with propriety. And that shows what good it does."

" Perhaps it does."

"Of course it does, whether you can see it or not; and I am willing to study for it by day and night."

"I should think it was about enough to study by day, and let the nights go," added James, demurely.

"There is where we don't think alike again. It would take me a long time to master this grammar, if I should study only my leisure moments in the daytime. I have used up from two to three hours over it every night of late."

"Just like you, Abe."

"Just like every poor fellow like me, who must do so, or know little or nothing. Dr. Franklin carried a book in his pocket, to study when he could, and he kept one by his side in the printing-office to read every minute he had to spare."

"How do you know that? Was you there?" and Nelson's roguishness appeared in his expressive eye.

"Probably," answered Abraham, in the same vein of remark.

"But did you ever read the Life of Dr. Franklin?"

"Certainly, several years ago; and if he had not done just what you think is quite foolish, he would have made candles all his life."

"And that would be sheddin' *light* on the world, I 'm sure," said Nelson, with an attempt at punning. "Lucky that somebody was willin' to make candles."

"And more lucky that Franklin was willing to improve his leisure hours in study," added Abraham. "This country is under great obligations to him."

"Well, you are talking about something that I don't understand, and so I —"

"Ah, Mr. Garland," said Abraham, rising from his seat, and stopping short the conversation, as an acquaintance entered with a friend. It was a little after eleven o'clock, A. M.

"Mr. Lincoln, this is Richard Yates, whom I have invited to see you," said Mr. Garland.

"Glad to see him," responded Abraham, extending his hand, which Richard grasped with his wonted cordiality.

This was Richard Yates, who has since been a very prominent statesman of Illinois, filling many offices with honor to himself. He has recently been Governor of the State. He was several years younger than Abraham. The fact was, the people of New Salem were proud of their "storekeeper," and they frequently took their visitors there to see him. This was the case with Mr. Garland.

"Come, Richard," he said, "I'll go over and introduce you to a fine young fellow we have here, — a smart, genial, active young fellow, and we'll be sure to have a good time." This was precisely the view that most of the people of New Salem had of Abraham. Sometimes these visits with strangers were a great annoyance and interruption to him. They liked him too well for the most advantageous improvement of his time. He thought too much of his leisure moments for study to submit without misgivings to so many interruptions. Still his good sense, urbanity, courtesy, and desire to treat every person with respect always triumphed.

He was soon engaged in close conversation with Yates upon various subjects, and while they were talking, Nelson left for home. Mr. Garland, also, excused himself, and left his young friend to be entertained by Abraham.

The dinner-time arrived before they were aware that nearly an hour had passed since they were introduced to each other. Abraham invited his new acquaintance to dine with him, and they proceeded to the house where he boarded, — a low, rough, log-house.

"Aunt Lizzie," said Abraham, "I have brought some company home to dinner."

"I'm glad of it, Abe, if you'll take me as you find me," replied the old lady, addressing her remark partly to Abraham, and partly to the visitor.

"No apologies are necessary," said Richard.

"No, none at all," added Abraham.

The dinner was on the table, and it was a very plain one. There was a plenty of bread, and milk enough for the company, and the addition of another bowl and spoon provided a dinner for visitor and all.

There were quite a number members of the family, boarders and children, and the aged matron waited upon the table, pouring the milk, and passing a brimming bowl to each. When Abraham was waited upon, by some mishap, his bowl slipped and rolled over upon the floor, dashing it to pieces, and covering the floor with its contents.

"O dear me!" exclaimed the old lady, in great trouble; "that was all my fault."

"Perhaps not," said Abraham.

"It surely was," she answered. "I am so careless."

"Well, Aunt Lizzy, we 'll not discuss whose fault it is," continued Abraham; "only if it don't trouble you, it don't trouble me."

"That 's you, Abe, sure," replied Aunt Lizzy. "You 're ready to comfort a body."

"A very good trait," said Richard, who was both amused and enlightened by the accident.

"Never mind, Aunt Lizzy," continued Abraham, "you have the worst of it; but I am really sorry that your bowl is broken. I don't care so much for the milk, as there is a plenty more where that came from. Much worse things happen sometimes."

By this time Aunt Lizzy had another bowl filled for Abraham, and the company proceeded to eat their dinner, while the old lady gathered up the fragments of the broken bowl, and wiped up the floor.

Here Abraham exhibited a trait of character for which he was distinguished from boyhood. He disliked to make trouble for any one, and wanted to see all persons at ease. Hence he was accommodating, never disposed to find fault, inclined to overlook the mistakes and foibles of others. Also, his readiness to assist the needy, and comfort the distressed and unfortunate, proceeded in part from this quality. It was made up of gentlemanly bearing, affability, generosity, and a true regard for the welfare and happiness of others. A rare character is this, though it is always needed, and is popular wherever it is appreciated.

We were absorbed in the discussion of Abraham and Nelson about the grammar, and were interrupted by the arrival of Richard, in consequence of which the conversation was broken off. We will only add, that Abraham became a very good grammarian by dint of perseverance. He did not cast aside the old grammar until he had mastered it, and it was all accomplished while he was the most faithful clerk that the store in New Salem ever had. He found time enough at odd moments during the day, and took enough out of his sleeping hours at night, within the space of a few months, to acquire all the knowledge of grammar that he ever possessed.

We should say, however, that his companion, William Greene, rendered him assistance in this study. William had some knowledge of grammar, and he cheerfully aided Abraham all that he could. The latter always said that William taught him grammar, although William still affirms "that he seemed to master it, as it were, by intuition."

It is probable that this old grammar laid the foundation, in part, of Abraham's future character. It taught him the rudiments of his native language, and thus opened the golden gate of knowledge. There is much in his experience at this point to remind us of that of Alexander Murray, the world-renowned linguist. His father was too poor to send him to school, or to provide him with books. The Bible and a catechism containing the alphabet were all the volumes in the family, and the latter Alexander was not allowed to see except on the Sabbath. During the week his father would draw the letters on the back of an old wool-card "with the black end of an extinguished heather-stem or root, snatched from the fire." In this way he learned the alphabet, and became a reader. At twelve years of age a friend presented him with a copy of Salmon's Grammar, which he mastered in an incredibly short period; and here commenced his progress in earnest. He borrowed a Latin grammar, and mastered it. Then a French grammar was studied with success. Then the Greek was taken in hand, and thus on till all the Oriental and Northern languages were familiar to him. And the study of Salmon's Grammar laid the foundation for all this. That was the key to the vast treasures of knowledge that were opened before him. By making himself master of that, he unlocked the temple of wisdom.

And so the grammar that Abraham studied exerted a great influence upon his character and destiny.

XXI.

CAPTAIN IN THE BLACK-HAWK WAR.

EARLY in the following spring the Black-Hawk War broke out, and the Governor of Illinois called for four regiments of volunteers.

"I shall enlist," said Abraham to his intimate friend and companion, William Greene, as soon as the news reached New Salem.

"So shall I, if you do," answered William. He was several years younger than Abraham.

"Well, I shall do it. Black Hawk is one of the most treacherous Indians there is, and I hope he will be shot. It is not more than a year ago, nor hardly that, that he entered into a treaty to keep his people on the other side of the Mississippi, and now he has crossed to make war on the whites."

"Just like an Indian," replied William. "The only way to keep them in their place is to show them no quarter."

"I don't know about that, though I am certain that we have got to fight Black Hawk to save ourselves. He is a cunning, artful warrior, and determined to massacre all the whites he can."

"I 'm ready to fight him for one," continued William; "and what do you say to raising a company here?"

"I should like it, if we can."

"I think we can. We can try it, anyhow."

"Who will enlist, do you think?"

"Almost everybody; it 's only for thirty days, you know."

"Yes; but I don't believe that thirty days will finish the war. I shall go and enlist to-morrow, whether it is for thirty days or thirty months."

"And I 'll go with you; and then we 'll see what can be done about raising a company."

"We shall have to get permission to do that," said Abraham.

"It will be given fast enough. Let us see about it when we enlist."

Recruiting-offices were opened in various places, though there was none at New Salem. Abraham expected to go to a neighboring town to enlist. But the subject was talked over that night, and it was concluded to apply for the privilege of raising a whole company in New Salem, in which case a recruiting-office would be opened there.

Abraham put his whole soul into the work. He conferred with his employer, and the latter readily released him from further engagements to him, that he might gratify his patriotic desires. A general enthusiasm was inspired in consequence, and the whole town became fired with military ardor. Enlistments progressed rapidly. Abraham's example, in being the first one to enlist, became the theme of remark, and it encouraged others to enroll their names in that time of peril. Nearly every one of his companions were foremost among the patriots. Within a few days the company was full.

Now the choice of officers must be decided, — a very important part of the enterprise, — much more important, in some respects, than the enlistments. The efficiency of the company would depend, in a great measure, upon its officers.

"There 's no question about it," said the father of young Greene, "Abe is altogether the best man for captain." This was not said in Abraham's presence, but was addressed to a number of the company.

"That 's it," answered a number of voices. The suggestion was adopted at once.

"I doubt whether he 'll accept," suggested one. "If he 'll serve, he can have every vote."

"Of course he can," said William. "Every man will be proud to make him captain; but he must n't know it till we choose him."

"Why ? " inquired one of the number.

"Because he 'll declare right up and down that he won't serve, if we tell him what we are going to do. He 's so modest, that he 'll think somebody else will do much better."

"Well, then, you must keep the matter close," said William's father, "but have a fair understanding among yourselves. Whisper the matter about, so that every vote will be right."

"And what if he won't accept then?" asked one of the aforesaid speakers.

"He must; we won't let him off anyhow, when he is elected. We will press him into the service," answered William.

Thus the matter was discussed and arranged, and Abraham was kept in the dark as to their intentions. The time for electing officers was appointed. More than once Abraham conversed with some of his companions about the fitness of this and that man for an office; but he did not dream of their purpose to give him the command of the company. His companions amused themselves over their success in keeping the purpose of the volunteers a secret.

The election took place, and every vote was cast for Abraham as captain. He was taken by surprise. He scarcely knew what to think or say. He was on the point of declining to serve; but the rousing cheers that arose drowned his voice. At length, however, he was assured that the company would not allow him to decline, and he very reluctantly consented to command them.

"Captain Lincoln, your honor!" said William Greene, bowing to him, in a humorous way, after his election.

"None of your fun at my expense," replied Abraham, who received the greeting with the same good feeling with which it was tendered

"We shall have the *tallest* captain," suggested another.

"In more senses than one, too," added William. with as roguish a twinkle of the eye as was ever witnessed.

Thus the affair passed off pleasantly, and no military company was ever more harmonious and happy in the choice of a captain, than was this company at New Salem. The truth was, they were proud of their young captain.

Of course his promotion was the subject of much conversation in the town, and some rather large stories were told about his abilities. Among them was the following, which was no larger than the facts warranted, though it seemed extravagant to the person addressed. Young Greene was in conversation with a stranger to Abraham, and Greene said, "He is the strongest man in Illinois."

"I don't believe that," the stranger replied; and he named some one who was stronger, in his opinion.

"How much will he lift?" asked Greene.

"He'll lift a barrel of flour."

"Abe will lift two, if he could get hold of them."

"Ha! ha! ha!" laughed the man. "You can tell a greater story than I can."

"Great story or not, I will bet that Abe will lift a barrel of whiskey holding forty gallons, and drink out of the bunghole."

"Worse yet," replied the man. "I'll bet he can't do any such thing."

"What will you bet?"

"I'll bet a good hat; and we'll have him try right off, if he will."

"Agreed," said Greene. The truth was, he had seen Abraham do this very thing, minus the drinking part, so that he knew he should win.

Without delay they proceeded to the store where Abraham was, and made known their errand.

"I don't think much of the betting part," said Abraham, "but I guess I'll help William out of the affair, though he won't have a chance to wear the hat yet awhile, if he is going to war with me."

"Well, if you can do what he says you can, I want to see it," said the man.

"You shall have the privilege," answered Abraham.

At once he proceeded to perform the feat, and accomplished it with seeming ease. The barrel was raised, as another man might lift a ten-gallon keg, and a quantity of liquor taken from the bunghole.

"There it is!" exclaimed Greene. "But that is the first dram I ever saw you drink in my life, Abe."

The words had scarcely escaped his lips, before

Abraham sat down the barrel, and spirted the whiskey that was in his mouth upon the floor, at the same time replying, "And I have n't drank that, you see."

Greene burst into a hearty laugh at this turn of the affair, and added, "You are bound to let whiskey alone, Abe."

And this same Greene writes to us: "That was the only drink of intoxicating liquor I ever saw him take, and that he spirted out on the floor."

The stranger was satisfied, as well as astonished. He had never seen the like before, and he doubted whether he ever should again. He did not know that the whole life-discipline through which the young captain had passed was suited to develop muscular strength. Probably he did not care, since there was the actual deed.

We are interested in it mostly for the determination it showed to reject whiskey. The act was in keeping with all his previous temperate habits.

On the evening after this affair, Abraham was alone with his friend William Greene, who won the aforesaid hat, and he said to him, "William, are you in the habit of betting?"

"No; I never bet before in my life, never."

"Well, I never would again, if I was you. It is what unprincipled men will do, and I would set my face against it."

"I did n't see anything very bad in this bet," said William.

"All bets are alike," answered Abraham, "though you may not have any bad motives in doing it."

"I only wanted to convince the man that you could lift the barrel."

"I know it; but I want you should promise me that you will never bet again. It is a species of gambling, and nothing is meaner than that."

"I don't suppose I ever shall do it again."

"I want you should promise me that you won't," continued Abraham, with increased emphasis. "It will please your mother to know of so good a resolution."

"I will promise you, Abe," answered William, grasping his hand, while tears glistened in his eyes. And there was true seriousness in this transaction, more than might appear to the reader at first view. The youth who thus pledged himself to Abraham writes to us now, in his riper years: "On that night, when alone, I wept over his lecture to me, and I have so far kept that solemn pledge."

The New Salem company went into camp at Beardstown, from whence, in a few days, they marched to the expected scene of conflict. When the thirty days of their enlistment had expired, however, they had not seen the enemy. They were disbanded at Ottawa, and most of the volunteers returned. But a new levy being called for, Abraham re-enlisted as a private. Another thirty days expired, and the war was not over. His regiment was disbanded, and again, the third time, he volunteered. He was determined to serve his country as long as the war lasted. Before the third term of his enlistment had expired, the battle of Bad Axe was fought, which put an end to the war.

He returned home. "Having lost his horse, near where the town of Janesville, Wisconsin, now stands, he went down Rock River to Dixon in a canoe. Thence he crossed the country on foot to Peoria, where he again took canoe to a point on the Illinois River, within forty miles of home. The latter distance he accomplished on foot."

One who served under him in the New Salem company writes, that he was a universal favorite in the army, that he was an efficient, faithful officer, watchful of his men, and prompt in the discharge of duty, and that his courage and patriotism shrank from no dangers or hardships.

XXII.

PLANS AND PROGRESS.

IT was pleasant for Lincoln to be with his old friends again, and they did not fail to express their interest in his welfare. Many of them delighted to show him honor by calling him Captain Lincoln. It was a mark of respect which they loved to show, as they thought of his patriotism and courage. His boon companions, however, called him by the old name Abe. But there was a higher honor in reserve for him. No sooner had he returned from the war than they began to plan for his promotion.

"Going to send you to the Legislature," said his old friend Greene to him one day.

"Send *me* to the Legislature!" exclaimed Lincoln, with wonder beaming all over his face.

"Yes, *you;* and you need n't be so astonished about it. Perhaps you 'll be a member of Congress yet."

"But you are joking. Nobody but you young fellows can be thinking of such a thing."

"I am not joking; and, moreover, I know that

older persons than we are thinking of such a thing."

"But it was only yesterday that I heard John T. Stuart, Colonel Taylor, and Peter Cartwright named as candidates."

"All that may be, and there may be a half-dozen other candidates; but we are going to run you against the whole batch, unless you positively decline."

"You are crazy, William, and all the rest of you who entertain such a thought. What! run me, nothing but a strapping boy, against such men of experience and wisdom! Come, now, no more of your gammon."

"Then you won't believe me?"

"I did n't say so."

"Well, believe it or not, you will be waited upon by older persons than I am, to get your consent."

And, sure enough, he was waited upon by several of the most influential citizens of New Salem within twenty-four hours thereafter, to ask his consent to run as a candidate for the Legislature.

"It will only subject me to ridicule," he said.

"Why so?" inquired one of the number.

"For the folly of running against such men as Stuart and Cartwright."

"Not if you beat them."

"That is impossible. I should not expect to be elected, if I should consent to be a candidate."

"I don't know about that," answered one; "we expect to elect you."

"But I have lived in the county only nine months, and am known only in New Salem, while the other candidates are known in every part of the county. Besides, it is only a few days before the election, and there is little time to carry your measures."

"Very true; but there is a principle involved in your nomination, and we shall sustain that, whether you are elected or not."

Here was a point of importance. There were no distinct political parties then in the State, as there are now. But there were "Jackson men," "Clay men," "Crawford men," and "Adams men." Abraham was a "Clay man," while the majority vote of the county, at the previous presidential election, was cast for Jackson. In these circumstances there was little prospect that the young candidate would be elected. There were as many as eight candidates in all, but none of them represented the principles of the "Clay men" so fully as Abraham.

Suffice to say that Abraham at last yielded very reluctantly, and became a candidate. He was not elected; but his popularity may be learned from the fact that he stood next to the successful candidate, and only a few votes behind him. "His own precinct, New Salem, gave him 277 votes in a poll of 284," — all but 7. No one was more surprised than Abraham himself. Although he was not elected, yet, in the circumstances, it was a great triumph.

"We'll do it next time," said his old friend Greene. "You see I'm not quite so near crazy as you thought I was," referring to their former conversation.

"I must confess that the result is much better than I expected." This was very true; for his modesty and humble view of himself always modified his anticipations of personal distinction,—a very good trait of character, and necessary to success.

"Prepare for a great triumph next time, Abe, for we shall certainly win it." And they did, as we shall see.

But we were speaking of what happened after Lincoln returned from the Black-Hawk War. The result of the aforesaid election—277 votes out of 284 votes in New Salem cast for him—showed that the people of the town were decidedly his friends. He could not doubt it longer. A majority of them were "Jackson men," and yet they voted for him, a "Clay man."

"I would remain here if I had any employment," he said to his old friend Greene, who knew that he was thinking of going elsewhere to find business.

"But you must stay here," replied Greene.

"There is no *must* about it, if there is no work for me," answered Lincoln.

"There 'll be enough that you can do, only take time for it; the world was n't made in a minute."

"No; I suppose it took about six days, and if I can find employment in that time, I shall be satisfied."

"I 'll tell you what to do Abe, — STUDY LAW: you 're just the man for it."

"Whew! I should laugh to see myself trying to make a lawyer."

"Why not be one, I should like to know?"

"For the very good reason, that I have n't brains enough."

"Just what I thought you would say. You are altogether too sparing of good opinions of yourself. You 've more brains than half the lawyers in Illinois."

"Perhaps that is n't saying much," replied Abraham, laughing; "although it is a pretty handsome compliment on your part. Much obliged."

"Well, compliment or not, I have heard a good many people say that you ought to be a lawyer."

"And I have heard one propose that I be a blacksmith; and I suppose I could swing a sledge-hammer equal to any of them. And, seriously, I have had some thoughts of choosing that trade."

"And throw away your talents? Any fool could be a blacksmith."

"By no means. No man can be successful in anything unless he is industrious, and has common sense, and a good share of perseverance."

"That's so, I s'pose; but a blacksmith is the last thing I would be, if I were in your place. I would like to know who ever suggested such an idea to you."

"My father, several years ago; and less than five years ago I came within an ace of putting his advice into practice. I almost decided to go at it for life."

"Ha! ha! ha!" laughed his friend, heartily. "Would n't you cut a dash, doffing a leathern apron, and blowing the blacksmith's bellows, like another Jake Smuttyface, as they used to call Jake Tower."

"An honest calling," answered Lincoln; "and that is the main thing. A lawyer can look a little more spruce than a son of Vulcan, to be sure; but a blacksmith can be just as upright, if not a little more so."

"And what do you mean by 'a little more so'?" asked Greene.

"Why, don't you know that nearly everybody suspects lawyers of trickery, — doing anything for a fee, blowing hot or cold for the sake of a case, — shielding the meanest culprits as readily as they do the best men, — and all that sort of thing?"

"Not quite so bad as that, Abe. I know that lawyers are not over particular, and that is true of a good many folks who are not lawyers. If you won't follow a calling because there are scapegraces in it, you will not choose one right away."

"Perhaps so; but no man has any more right to defend the wrong because he is a lawyer than he has because he is a blacksmith, in my way of thinking."

"I give it up, Abe; you 've got the case already, and I am more convinced than ever that you ought to study law."

"That is, if you are judge and jury," responded Lincoln. "But I don't understand why it is that people are determined I shall be a lawyer. As many as ten months ago, two or three people gave me the same advice, though I thought they were half in joke."

"Well, Abe, perhaps you 'll get your eyes open, if you live long enough, to see what you ought to be," said Greene, in a strain of pleasantry. "Not many folks live that have to go to their neighbors to find out what they are. By the time you are *seven feet* high, perhaps you will understand."

"I should think I was pretty near that now, by what people say," archly replied Lincoln.

"I think you are in a fair way to be, if you keep on."

"And I shall be a lawyer by that time, and not before." And here they parted.

Lincoln had no intention of being a lawyer, after all that his friends had suggested. He had no confidence in his abilities for that profession. Indeed, he could not see how a young man reared as he was could expect to enter upon such a calling.

Yet he longed for some permanent pursuit,—a life-vocation. He did not like this going from one thing to another, and he only did it from sheer necessity. He believed that a young man should choose a calling, and stick to it with unwearied devotion, if he would make anything in the world. He wanted to do this; but what should he choose? He was perplexed, troubled, and the more so, because admiring friends advised him to do what he really supposed was beyond his ability. He underrated his talents, (a very good failing,) and all the time thought that others were overrating them. Few youth and young men suffer in this way. They are more apt to injure themselves by too exalted views of their talents. Some of the veriest simpletons esteem themselves as the wisest and greatest men. Ignorance is more likely to be vain and proud than ripe talents and learning. True knowledge is humble. Great talents are marked by humility. And so young Lincoln did not stand so high in his own estimation as he did in the estimation of others. This was the case with Sir Humphrey Davy, Nathaniel Bowditch, Arkwright, Franklin, Washington, and many others. From their youth, they were devoid of that vain self-confidence which many shallow-brained people possess.

Lincoln did not leave town. In company with another man, he bought the store of Offutt, and went into business again. It was at this stage of his career that he adopted a plan of improvement worthy of notice. As usual, he devoted all his spare moments to reading, and now he adopted the plan of writing out a synopsis of each book he read. This would fix the contents of the volume in his mind, and prove far more profitable. There can be no doubt that this exercise exerted a most beneficial influence upon his habits of thought and study. It is a practice that the young generally ought to adopt, as necessary to the highest improvement.

Within a few months, however, he sold out to his partner, believing that they could not make the enterprise profitable.

He had but just relinquished the store business, when he unexpectedly met John Calhoun of Springfield. Since that time, Calhoun has been notorious for his efforts to enslave Kansas. He was President of the Lecompton Constitutional Convention. But when he met Abraham, at the time mentioned, he was engaged in a more legitimate and honorable business, — that of Surveyor for Sangamon County.

"Try your hand at surveying," said Calhoun.

"I know nothing about it."

"Learn then."

"How can I do that."

"Easy enough, if you want to do it."

"I do want to do it. I think I should like the business, if I could qualify myself for it."

"You can, and in a few weeks, too. I will loan you Flint and Gibson, the authors you will want to study, and you can provide yourself with a compass and chain, and I will render you any assistance I can."

"You are very kind, Mr. Calhoun, and I will do the best I can. Your generous offer shall not come to nothing for the want of my trying."

"You 'll make a good surveyor, I 'm sure of that, and find plenty of business. And, what is more, I will depute to you that portion of my field contiguous to New Salem."

"It is more than I could expect of you," said Lincoln. "I could not ask so great a favor."

"Take it without asking," said Calhoun, in a jolly way. "I have much more than I can do, and I am glad to give you a portion of the county. The great influx of immigrants, and the consequent entry of government lands, has given me more than my hands full."

"I shall be glad to accept your offer as soon as I am qualified for the business."

"The bargain is closed, then, and in four weeks you can be surveying, if you 're a mind to," said Calhoun.

"I shall have a mind to, if that is all," replied Lincoln; "and with a thousand thanks, too, for your assistance. It is worth all the more to me now, because I am thrown out of business."

"Well, this will make business enough for you, and it needs a long-legged, tough, wiry fellow like you to do it well. This is a great country for surveyors."

"But shall I not need to take some lessons of you in the field?"

"If you please. It will be a capital idea, and you are welcome to all I can aid you any time you will come where I am. It will give you a sweat to keep up with me."

"Perhaps so," replied Lincoln, looking very much as if he did not believe it. The actual experiment proved that the sweat was given to the other party.

Lincoln sat down to this new study with a keen relish, and, in a short time, having been some with Mr. Calhoun in the field, he was prepared to set up the business of a surveyor. With his usual thoroughness and energy, he engaged in the business, and proved himself a workman that needeth not be ashamed.

Now he had an employment, and a plenty to do. The prospect was, that he might follow this pursuit through life, and probably his old friend Greene concluded that an end was put to his becoming a lawyer.

For more than a year he continued to survey without interruption, and won quite a reputation in the business. A circumstance, narrated in the next chapter, brought an unexpected change.

XXIII.

SUCCESS AND ITS RESULTS.

IT was the summer of 1834, two years after Lincoln was candidate for the Legislature. In Illinois, representatives were elected every two years, so that another election was close by. August was the month for it.

Lincoln was not forgotten. Since the last election he had become well known in the county. He had been to war, and distinguished himself. He was the first to enlist and the last to leave. A degree of military glory was attached to his name. Then he was a successful surveyor. No one in that line of business was more correct than he. In this regard, his prospects were very much better than they were two years before.

"We shall make a sure thing of it this time, Abe," said his associate, Greene.

"Whether you do or not is not of much consequence to me," he replied. "I have a good business now, and am satisfied."

"You've been consulted, I s'pose, before this about it?"

"Yes, some time ago."

"Consented, of course?"

"Yes."

"Enough said. That's all we want of you: we can do the rest.'

"So you thought before."

"There's more reason to think so now."

"How so?"

"You've been to war," said Greene, with a significant glance of the eye. "You know they make great men out of military heroes."

"You mean those of them who possess something to make greatness out of it."

"Just as you please. But don't you want the office, Abe?"

"I am not particular about it. I do not want it enough to work for it. If my friends see fit to give it to me, I shall accept it, and do the best I can."

"I didn't expect you would ever make a politician, Abe; there's not cheat enough about you for that. But, really now, I should think you would jump at the chance?"

"Chance of what? the chance of getting beat?"

"No; the chance of becoming a legislator."

"Time enough to *jump* at that when I get it."

"It's as certain as the rule of three, Abe."

"We can settle that point after election."

"Well, when you get there, remember that I am a 'Clay man' as well as yourself."

"As to that, we are all *clay* men, if the Bible is true, and I expect it would be much better for us to keep it more in mind"; and there was not so much seriousness in this remark as might at first seem. Lincoln always had much dry wit about him, that kept oozing out.

"But, to speak soberly," he continued, "there is too much trickery and underhanded work among politicians to suit me."

"If there is nothing worse than that," replied Greene, "we are better off than I think we are."

"I should think that was bad enough."

"True; but rascality is worse, and there is plenty of that. That is one reason we want to send you to the Legislature. We shall be sure of one decent fellow"; and this last sentence was closed with an uproarious laugh. Greene actually enjoyed complimenting Lincoln, to see the workings of his modesty. There was nothing that would put the damper on him so quickly as to "thrust a compliment into the front door," as somebody has said. Greene knew this, and so he rather enjoyed it. At the same time he honored him more on this account.

. . . . .

The day of election came, — a bright, warm, pleasant day in August, — and the voters of the county improved it. There was a large vote polled; and, as the friends of Lincoln anticipated, he was elected by a large majority. At nightfall, enough was learned of the ballot to place his election beyond a doubt.

His friends were jubilant. His intimate associates were full of glee. They waited upon him that night, to congratulate him upon the result.

"You see it is done, Abe, just as I told you," said Greene. "And now you must treat."

"Of course he must," said Nelson, looking towards his companions, and the very tone of his voice indicating that he knew he would do no such thing.

"Such times don't come every day," continued Greene, "and you must treat."

"Treat you well, I suppose," answered Lincoln, making another use of their language.

"Yes, it will be treating us well to take us over to the tavern, and provide all the whiskey we want."

"That would be the worst kind of treatment that I could give you. I will treat you better than that, for you deserve it after conferring such honor upon me."

"Come on, then; we go in for good treatment, Abe," said Nelson; and two of them took hold of him, one at each arm, to march him along.

"I shall do no such thing," exclaimed Lincoln. "I'll treat you with a plenty to eat, and tea or coffee to drink, but I won't treat you with rum or whiskey. Look here, William, — you go in for consistent and honest politicians; now give me a chance. Let me begin to-day."

"After that treat," answered Nelson, not waiting for William to reply.

"It will have to come before, if ever," said Lincoln. "Rum has made more politicians mean than anything else."

"But we won't ask you to drink, only treat us," said one. "You'll never be Governor till you can treat."

"I never want to be, if that is necessary to it. I shall not do it, you may depend on that."

"Then I s'pose we must give it up, and go dry," said Nelson to his companions; "for when Abe says a thing, he means it."

"That's a fact," added Greene. "Stick to your principles, Abe, like a good one, and we'll honor you for it. We are not very dry, after all."

Their vain attempt to get a drink out of their friend on this occasion did not diminish their regard for him. Indeed, they made the request more to annoy him than anything; for they had never had an opportunity to drink with him. He always declined this custom of friendly intercourse, and they expected he would at this time. They honored him all the more for it, too, in their hearts. It was a regard for principle and purity, and an exhibition of decision and firmness, that won their respect.

We pass over the interim to the assembling of the Legislature in December, and shall devote neither space nor time to that, except to narrate the following fact.

It was during the sitting of the Legislature that Lincoln decided to study law, without waiting to become seven feet high. It was on this wise.

He was thrown much into the society of Hon John T. Stuart, an eminent lawyer, and one of the most distinguished men of the State. This gentleman was a close observer, and he soon discovered that young Lincoln possessed unusual talents. He had no doubt that he would make his mark, if he could have the opportunity; so he embraced a favorable time to advise him about studying law.

"Have you ever thought of studying law?" Mr. Stuart inquired, in a delicate manner.

"Never, though the subject has been named to me by others," replied Lincoln.

"And why have you not entertained the suggestion favorably?"

"Because I have not talents enough to warrant such a decision; and then I have no means, even if I had the talents."

"Perhaps you have too exalted views of the abilities required. Let us see. Is there anything in the law so intricate as to demand superior talents? Does it require more ability than medicine or theology? No, I think you will say. And then, if it did, perhaps the future will reveal that you possess the talents for it."

"But then, a poor fellow like me, with no friends to aid, can hardly think of going through a long course of study."

"It is not very long after all, and there need not be much expense about it, except for your board and clothes."

"How can that be?"

"You can read law by yourself, working at your business of surveyor enough to board and clothe yourself, and in less than three years be admitted to the bar."

"But books are expensive, especially law-books."

"Very true; but that difficulty is easily remedied. You shall be welcome to my library. Come as often as you please, and carry away as many books as you please, and keep them as long as you please."

"You are very generous, indeed. I could never repay you for such generosity."

"I don't ask any pay, my dear sir," responded Mr. Stuart, shaking his sides with laughter. "And if I did, it would be pay enough to see you pleading at the bar."

"I am almost frightened at the thought of appearing there," added Lincoln.

"You 'd soon get over your fright, I reckon, and bless your stars that you followed the advice of John T. Stuart."

"I dare say."

"Only think of it," continued Mr. Stuart, "a brighter prospect is before you than hundreds of distinguished men enjoyed in early life, on account of the advantages offered to you. You are a 'Clay man,' and you now have the offer of better opportunities to rise than he had when he left his mother's log-cabin. All the schooling he ever enjoyed was in his boyhood, when he went to school to Peter Deacon, in a log school-house, without a window or floor. All the learning he acquired after that was got by industry and perseverance, improving every leisure moment, and extending his studies far into the night."

"I don't see but he had as good advantages in his early life as I did," interrupted Lincoln.

"That is so; and there is much in your history that reminds me of his. I suppose that is what suggested the comparison to me. You have a right to be a 'Clay man.' One would scarcely have thought, when he was seen riding his mother's old horse, without a saddle, and with a rope for a bridle, on his way to mill with a grist on the horse's back, that he — 'The Mill-Boy of the Slashes,' as he was called — would become one of the most renowned men of the land."

"That is so; and I admire the man for his noble efforts to rise in the world. He made himself just what he became," said Lincoln.

"And that is what you, and every other young man, will do, if you ever make a mark. 'Self-made, or never made,' is the adage. It is of little consequence what advantages a youth possesses, unless he is disposed to improve them; and I am almost of the opinion that it matters but little how few the privileges a young man enjoys, if he only has the energy and industry to make the most of them."

"And the *ability*, you might add," said Lincoln.

"Perhaps so, if you choose. But the history of our country abounds with examples of these self-made men, as poor and unknown as Henry Clay was. But now I must go; remember my counsel, and decide right."

"Many thanks for your interest," answered Lincoln. "I shall certainly ponder the subject, and feel grateful to you, whether I decide as you recommend or not."

He did ponder the subject. He inferred that he must possess some qualifications for the legal profession when such a man as Mr. Stuart advised him as above. The counsel of Mr. Stuart made more impression upon him than the previous advice of all his friends. Soon after the legislature adjourned, he decided to become a lawyer; and we shall proceed to show how it was done.

XXIV.

WORKING AND WINNING.

"GOOD, Abe!" exclaimed William Greene, when the news of Lincoln's decision to study law had spread through the village; "glad to hear that you have taken up with my advice, and are going to study law."

"I did n't know that it was according to your advice," said Lincoln.

"Did n't?"

"No, I am sure I did not."

"Months ago I talked with you about it in the store, and tried to beat it into your head that you ought to be a lawyer, and you finally came to the decision that you should be one about the time you were seven feet high."

"O yes! I do remember it now," said Lincoln. "You see I did not wait to arrive at that stature of a man. I concluded that it would not make much difference if I did fall an inch short."

"Very like; but now I s'pose you 'll hive yourself up in the house and pore over your books, so that we shall see little more of you."

"Not quite so bad, though I shall be obliged to improve my time both at work and study. It looks like the greatest job I ever undertook."

"Perhaps it is; and it may turn out to be the most profitable one: I think it will. Hallo! if there ain't David! I wonder what is afoot now." Just at that time David Rittenhouse approached them, as they stood conversing in the street.

"You are just the persons I want to see," said David. "We want you to come over to our house to-morrow evening. Nat and his lady are on from the East, and we are goin' to have a little gatherin' there." Nathaniel (commonly called Nat) was David's brother, who lived in New England, and he had just returned to Illinois on a flying visit with his bride.

"Then Nat is married, is he?" inquired Greene.

"Yes; and I told him that we would get together to express our sympathy for him in his loss of liberty."

"Probably he takes his loss philosophically," said Lincoln.

"Certainly, he 's perfectly resigned to his fate, and I hardly think you will wonder when you see his pretty wife. I could be reconciled to his condition, I think."

"No doubt," replied Lincoln, dryly; "but whether *she* could be is another question."

"You are keen, Abe, to-day," said David, with a

laugh. "But come now, what do you say to coming over to our house to-morrow night? Can't take no for an answer."

"But you must, so far as I am concerned," answered Lincoln. "I 'm going to Springfield to-morrow, for my books, and back again."

"Let your books go for to-morrow, and let us have a good time for once. Nat will be off in three days."

"I should be glad to go, but it is impossible. I must forego all such pleasures now. The evenings are my best time for studying. And there is yet another thing, — I have n't a suit of clothes fit to wear on such an occasion."

"Fudge! your clothes are good enough. Wear those you have on, if you can't do better. The clothes don't make the man."

"That is all folly. You 'd be ashamed of me, if I appeared in such a dress. The fact is, I intended to have bought a new suit of clothes this season, but my decision to study law has made it necessary for me to economize; so I shall wear my old clothes for the present."

"And stay at home," interrupted David.

"I must stay at home, at any rate," replied Lincoln, "and buckle down to hard study when I am not at work, if I intend to do anything."

"*I* would n't do it for all the law in creation, and all the books that you could pile up in New Salem," said David.

"And there is just the difference between you and Abe," added Greene. "He takes to books, and you don't."

"I am as fond of society as either of you," said Lincoln; "but I must deny myself of this enjoyment, if I would succeed in my plans. It is pretty clear that I must do two things: I must practise economy of time and money, and be as industrious as possible."

"A solemn view of the future," said David, rather sarcastically.

"And a correct one, too, I guess," added Greene.

"Correct or not," said Lincoln, "it is the course I have marked out for myself, and I shall not deviate from it."

"David ought to understand that," responded Greene; "for when you make up your mind to a thing, you are as firm as the hills, — can't stir you a peg."

"Yes, I know that," said David, "and so I suppose that he cannot be prevailed upon to come to our house to-morrow night."

"Yes, you must understand it so," replied Lincoln, "although I should enjoy being there. I must go to Springfield to-morrow at any rate, and I sha'n't get home till late."

"I sha'n't urge you, Abe," continued David; "for it will do no good: all is, I 'm sorry we shall have to try and get along without you."

"That you can easily do," replied Lincoln,—"much more easily than I can walk to Springfield and back. There will be enough there without me."

This was only a specimen of his self-denial, and the decision with which he adhered to his purpose. He canvassed the whole subject in the beginning, and he resolved to spend no evenings in social entertainments. He saw that he must do it from sheer necessity, as he would be obliged to use up the night hours much more economically than the laws of health would permit. And now he was inflexible. His purpose was fixed, and no allurements or promises of pleasure could make him swerve a hair's breadth therefrom.

Springfield was twenty-two miles from New Salem, and yet Lincoln walked there and back on the day proposed. He made a long day of it, and a wearisome one, too. On the following evening Greene called upon him, to learn how he made it.

"What!" he exclaimed. "Did you bring all these books home in your arms?" They were Blackstone's Commentaries, in four volumes.

"Yes; and read one of the volumes more than half of the way," Lincoln replied. "Come, now, just examine me on that first volume."

He had a faculty of perusing a volume when he was walking, and he often did it. He gained time thereby.

"I don't see what you are made of, to endure so," continued Greene. "It would use me all up to carry such a load a quarter part of that distance."

"I am used to it, you know, and that makes the difference. But, come, just see what I know about the first part of that volume." And he passed the first volume to him.

"If you pass muster, you'll want I should admit you to the bar, I suppose," responded Greene, humorously. "That I shall be glad to do."

So he proceeded to examine Lincoln on the first volume; and he found, to his surprise, that he was well posted on every part of it that he had read. By his close attention, and the ability to concentrate his thoughts, he readily made what he read his own.

Thus Lincoln began and continued the study of law, alternating his time between surveying and study, going to Springfield for books as often as it was necessary, and often pursuing his reading of law far into the night. People were universally interested in his welfare, and all predicted that he would make his mark by and by.

With such devotion did he employ his time in study and manual labor, denying himself of much that young men generally consider essential, that we might say of him, as Cicero said of himself: "What others give to public shows and entertainments, to festivity, to amusements, nay, even to mental and bodily rest, I give to study and philosophy." Even when he was engaged in the fields surveying, his thoughts were upon his books, so that much which he learned at night was fastened in his mind by day. He might have adopted the language of Cicero concerning himself: "Even my leisure hours have their occupation."

After Lincoln had been studying some time, he had a job at surveying, several miles from home. His employer was an ignorant man, rather inclined to hold literary men in contempt. At first he did not know that Lincoln was a prospective lawyer, but he soon found out.

"Allers up to somethin' that don't 'mount to nothin', these edicated men," said Holmes, for whom he was surveying. "I wish the wuthless crew of 'em were sent to the jumpin'-off place."

"That is rather of a hard wish," replied Lincoln; "why do you feel so about educated men?"

"'Cause they don't airn their salt. They jist screw their livin' out of other folks."

"How so?"

"By tryin' to live by their wits, and feelin' too big to dirty their hands with work."

"Does anybody work harder than Parson Jones, I should like to know."

"He don't work at all, my word for it. He jist totes about from place to place, and gets his bread and butter out of other people."

"Did he ever get any out of you, Mr. Holmes?" inquired Lincoln, rather rebukingly, as he did not like this unjust assault upon a good man.

"I'd be split if he did; I know too much to be come it on by him."

Parson Jones was a pioneer preacher, who performed a great amount of labor in his circuit, trusting to Providence to move the hearts of good people to support him; and they did it cheerfully. But Holmes hated him because he was a minister, and not a tiller of the soil as ignorant as himself. He was not a literary man by any means, but Holmes so regarded him.

"You have no reason to complain, then, if he has taken nothing from you," said Lincoln. "People generally are glad to support him for the good that he does."

"Fudge! He cares no more about people than I do, only to get his livin' out on 'em."

"I don't believe that. Society is much better in all this region in consequence of his labors. The trouble is, that you hate ministers"; and he would like to have said more, but he thought it was not best.

"Jist as I hate all yer larned folks, that are too lazy to work. 'Squire Bates is jist like the rest o' the crew."

"Then you don't believe in lawyers?"

"I'll bet I don't; they'll cheat ye out of your eyeteeth."

"But how would you get a legal claim to your section without them? Won't Lawyer Bates make out your papers?"

"Wall, y-i-s, I s'pose he will, if they are made out at all."

"Then you see that lawyers have their place to fill; and we should not know how to get along without them. Did you know that I am going to be a lawyer, Mr. Holmes?"

"My sakes!" exclaimed Holmes, with much surprise; "'t ain't so, is it?"

"It certainly is; I am now pursuing my studies."

"If that's the way yer study, I hain't no objections to that."

"I don't mean that I am studying to-day, while I am surveying; but I spend a part of my time in reading law, and work just enough to pay my way."

"Well, that's 'nuff sight better than many on 'em do; for they studies, and let's other folk's victual 'em. But du tell, Abe, ef you be's goin' into the lor business?"

"Why, yes, I am serious in all that I say. I have my books of Mr. Stuart, of Springfield, and shall go there for them as often as I want them. And when I become a lawyer, I shall stop surveying; so you must hurry up this business, if you expect me to perform it."

"Thar 't is, Abe; jist as I said; when folks takes to book larnin', they git above work."

"Not so, Mr. Holmes; no man can follow two callings with success. You know Dr. Franklin said, that we must not have 'too many irons in the fire.' I can't be a good lawyer and surveyor at the same time, and so when I am prepared to practise law, I must give my time to it. You can't be a good farmer and a good carpenter at once, can you?"

"I s'pose not; but how many weeks will yer be in gittin' into that ere lor business?"

"Weeks!" exclaimed Lincoln; "why, it will be several years before I do that, — at least two years, to do the best I can, and study half of the nights."

"I 'd see the lor in Ginny 'fore I 'd du it," replied Mr. Holmes.

Lincoln could not convince his ignorant employer that lawyers amount to much, but he was just as intent upon his profession for all that. Sometimes he was engaged days and weeks together in surveying, having only his nights in which to study; and then, again, he had both day and night to give to his books for a time. Nor did his interest abate in the least; it rather increased than otherwise. The longer he studied, the more deeply absorbed he became in his books. His robust physical constitution enabled him to endure hard toil both of body and mind, otherwise he would have broken down.

"I should rather be in prison, than to sit up nights studying as you do, and be at it at all other times you can," said David Rittenhouse to him.

"I really enjoy it, David."

"I can hardly credit it."

"Then you think I do not speak the truth?"

"O no, for no one ever suspects you of tellin' what is not true. I only meant to say, that I cannot understand it."

"We are not all constituted alike."

"Very few are made like you, Abe, in that respect. You rather have books than victuals or clothes, I should think, by your actions."

"I rather have *less* food and clothes, and more knowledge, if I can get it: that is about as strong a statement as the truth will bear."

"I have no doubt that your views are nearer right than mine, Abe, and I expect you will make a stir in the world."

"Nonsense, David; you can't talk without getting off your flattery. I hope time will convince you."

"I expect it will, and make me out a prophet, too," replied David, with a significant look.

Allusion is here made to an important fact. David could not understand how Abraham could possess such a love of knowledge as to lead him to forego all social pleasures, be willing to wear a threadbare coat, live on the coarsest fare, and labor hard all day, and sit up half the night, for the sake of learning. But there is just that power in the love of knowledge, and it was this that caused Lincoln to derive happiness from doing what would have been a source of misery to David. Some of the most marked instances of self-forgetfulness recorded are connected with the pursuit of knowledge. Archimedes was so much in love with the studies of his profession, that he frequently forgot his meals, and scarcely knew whether his garments were on his back or not. He was taking a bath when the idea was suggested that led to the accurate knowledge of the specific gravities of different bodies, and he is said to have rushed forth naked into the streets of Syracuse, exclaiming, "I HAVE FOUND IT! I HAVE FOUND IT!" Professor Heyne, of Göttingen, also, from his childhood possessed this unquenchable love of knowledge. His parents struggled with the most depressing poverty, and his father, who was a weaver, was often unable to provide bread for his large family. Heyne says, in his Memoirs of his own Life: "Want was the earliest companion of my childhood. I well remember the painful impressions made on my mind by witnessing the distress of my mother, when without food for her children. How often have I seen her, on a Saturday evening, weeping and wringing her hands, as she returned home from an unsuccessful effort to sell the goods which the daily and nightly toil of my father had manufactured." And yet, if he could get a book, he was content to run about barefoot and ragged. Later in life, when he was resolved to pursue his studies at all hazards, he actually suffered for the want of the necessaries of life, and allowed himself only two nights' sleep in a week. But he was happy only when he was engaged in the pursuit of knowledge. He preferred it, with poverty and hardship, to ignorance, with riches and ease, so all-inspiring is the love of knowledge.

Lincoln made rapid advancement in his studies, and became more enthusiastic therein every day. Week after week, and month after month, he continued them, interrupted only by his jobs at surveying, and going to the legislature. His journeys to Springfield, as often as it was necessary, constituted an interesting part of his programme. He enjoyed them, because they were a necessary means to an end.

And so he worked, and won. The reader may learn how well he progressed, from the fact that in about two years he was admitted to the bar, and Mr. Stuart received him as a partner in the practice of law. He saw marked talents and an honest purpose in his young friend, and he had high hopes of his success. His connection with Mr. Stuart, also, was creditable to Lincoln, since it was proof that he had done well, and promised to do better still.

We should stop the history at this point, and close at once with a brief summary of his after life; but there is one scene belonging to his later years that requires particular attention, because of its connection with an event already considered. It transpired after he was admitted to the bar, and we shall devote the closing chapter to it.

XXV.

THE TRAGEDY.

"A MAN killed!" shouted several voices, and the alarm rang along the tents.

"Where?" exclaimed one, rushing from a tent.

"Who?" cried out another, under great excitement.

"Seize the villain!"

"Who did it?"

"This way in a minute!"

"Where 's a constable?"

Thus the excited crowd cried out one after another, and all together running to and fro in great consternation, as they were aroused by the startling cry. Few understood what had happened, nor where the tragedy was; but the fearful cry ringing upon the night air assured them that some terrible crime had been perpetrated. It was at a camp-meeting in Menard County, Illinois; and the excitement broke up the meetings for a time, rendering night almost hideous with the shouts and cries of the excited and terrified people.

"Yonder!" shouted a young man, who seemed

to understand just where the fearful scene was. "He 's murdered!" and on he ran, scarcely knowing what his errand was.

"There 's been a fight," said another, "and a fellow is killed, — been stabbed right through the heart."

"O dear!" exclaimed a woman at the dreadful recital. "Who could do such a wicked thing?"

"Rum did it, madam," replied the man. "They were all drunk, and so they pitched into each other like so many tigers; and it is a burning shame that such things should be suffered at a camp-meeting."

"Indeed it is," added the woman; "but there are so many people who have n't the fear of God before their eyes, that we ought not to be surprised at anything. Who were they?"

"They were all young men, and so much the worse for that."

"Do you know any of them?"

"I heard one of them charging the deed upon Joe Armstrong; but my opinion is, that they were all too drunk to know who did it. There is so much confusion and noise that I could n't find out much about it."

By this time, many had discovered where the trouble was, and a crowd of people collected, with numerous inquiries about the affair, and officers to arrest the parties were loudly called for.

After the excitement had subsided, and the affair

was pretty well investigated, the following facts came out: — A few fast young men became intoxicated, and from hard words proceeded to harder blows. Angry passions raged more and more fiercely, until one of the number plunged a knife into the breast of another, and he fell dying to the ground, and soon ceased to breathe. One of the number charged the murder upon Joe Armstrong, declaring that he saw him inflict the blow; and so Joe was arrested, notwithstanding that he stoutly denied the charge.

The tidings of Joe's arrest travelled quickly to his native place, so that everybody there learned the facts in the case on the next day; and many were ready to believe that Joe was the murderer. He was the son of the Mr. Armstrong who gave Lincoln a home a few years before, as narrated in a former chapter.

Nearly all were disposed to rake over his past life, and cite every act of wickedness of which he had been guilty, magnifying them not a little in their excited state of mind. His difficulties with the boys of the neighborhood, his headstrong disposition, the "high scrapes" in which he had participated, and many other things, were brought up against him, and it all served to convince them that he was now a murderer.

It was not strange that the public mind, in its excited state, should thus pile upon the young man the sins of his youth. For this is usually the case.

When bad boys grow up to manhood, and are bad men, the evil deeds of their youth are usually brought up to set out the corruption of their later life. They cannot run away from their youthful sins, nor wipe them out, except by repentance and reformation. So Joe Armstrong had to meet the sins of his past life, at the same time that this great crime was charged upon his unrighteous manhood.

"I pity his good old mother," said Mr. Jones, who had been to see her. "It seems as if she could scarcely endure it, though she does not think that Joe is guilty of murder."

"Of course she would n't," answered his wife; "would n't a mother be likely to think her own son innocent of such a charge? Poor woman! If half of her good pious counsels had been treasured up in Joe's heart, or half of her prayers answered, he would not have come to such a sad end as this."

"I can scarcely see how it is that such good parents are so disappointed in their children," continued Mr. Jones. "They 've tried hard enough to make Joe what he ought to be. I 'm not sure but his father worried himself into his grave, and I 'm almost glad that he did n't live to see this day."

"And so am I," said his wife. "But his mother seems to think a deal of Joe; I have wondered at it sometimes. She never seemed to me to think he was any worse than other people's sons. I think she has been blinded to his true character."

"That is n't strange. It is natural for her to lean upon him, widow as she is, and to hope against hope, that he would become better as he grew older! And I pity her all the more for it."

Mr. Armstrong died two or three years after Lincoln had a home in the family, and Joe had professed to look after the farm and his mother since the day the good father was laid under the turf. He had served his mother better in her widowhood than most of the neighbors supposed, and much of the talk against him now arose from exaggerated accounts of his vicious practices. He was not half so bad as the stories represented him to be. The excitement was such that molecules of vice were magnified into mountains. But he was far from being a virtuous young man.

A bill was found against young Armstrong, and he was "bound over" for trial, and lodged in jail. It was a sorry day for him, as the reader will imagine, when the court bound him over under the charge of murder, and he was sent to prison. It was a still more sorrowful day for his mother, who had never dreamed of such an experience as this. But for her Christian hope, and her unshaken confidence in his innocence, she would have sunk under the crushing trial. As it was, she was bowed down with her weight of grief, fearing that he might be condemned, though he was not guilty. And perhaps, deep down in the secret of her heart, she feared, even against her belief in his innocence, that he might be guilty.

"You must obtain legal advice," said kind Mr. Jones to her, "and perhaps he may be saved yet."

"How can I, a poor widow, with not an extra dollar in the world, do that?" she replied. "I don't see but what he must be left to run his chance of having justice done him without a lawyer."

"But you must not give up to your feelings so. Now is the time to see what can be done, and I should be glad to assist you all I can."

"You are very kind, Mr. Jones, and your sympathy is worth everything to me in this hour of trial; and I should be glad to do anything that will save my boy; but I don't know what to do."

"You can go to Esquire A——, and tell him your circumstances and wants, and I have no doubt that he will advise you without charge. And then you should have an interview with your son at the earliest opportunity."

"Will they admit me to his cell for such an interview?"

"Certainly, under proper restrictions, and with reference to affording him a fair trial. I believe that Esquire A—— would cheerfully go with you for such an interview, and you will need to take a lawyer with you."

"Your kindness greatly encourages me, Mr. Jones. 'A friend in need is a friend indeed,' and I thank you a thousand times. May the Lord reward you for your sympathy for the widow and fatherless."

Mr. Jones went out silently, and an observer might have seen him brush a tear from his moistened eye as he closed the door.

Mrs. Armstrong decided to see what could be done for her boy. As soon as she could arrange matters at home, she determined to see Esquire A——, and do certain other things which the circumstances suggested. In these things, however, she was delayed, partly by duties at home, and partly by the fact that the trial was some weeks distant, and hence there was no special reason for haste. But just as she was on the point of executing her purpose, she received a letter running as follows: —

SPRINGFIELD, ILL., Sept. —, 18—.

DEAR MRS. ARMSTRONG: —

I have just heard of your deep affliction, and the arrest of your son for murder. I can hardly believe that he can be guilty of the crime alleged against him. It does not seem possible. I am anxious that he should have a fair trial at any rate; and gratitude for your long-continued kindness to me in adverse circumstances prompts me to offer my humble services gratuitously in his behalf. It will afford me an opportunity to requite, in a small degree, the favors I received at your hand, and that of your lamented husband, when your roof afforded me grateful shelter without money and without price.

Yours truly,

ABRAHAM LINCOLN.

"God be praised!" exclaimed Mrs. Armstrong, as tears of joy came to her relief; and, dropping upon her knees, she poured out her grateful feelings to God for this timely aid. It was the brightest hour she had seen since her dear boy was charged with murder. She felt that God was with her. She could now see his hand in all the past, and she began to hope that all would be well in future. Years before she sheltered the poor boy in her humble cabin, and now he had come to shelter her in his turn. Here was God. She could not doubt it. This was providence. She felt it in the very depths of her soul. She could see why it was that she befriended the poor youth when he was penniless. God's hand was in it to raise up a deliverer for her when the darkest hour of her life oppressed her soul. And she repeated over and over the sweet promise,—"He that watereth shall be watered also himself."

Mrs. Armstrong was now fully aroused from her despondency, and hope was revived in her heart. The cloud was breaking to her view. She resolved to do what she could.

No time was lost in having an interview with her son; she also communicated with her true friend, who proffered his services as above, and made haste to secure an impartial trial. At every step hope brightened. She became fully convinced that he was innocent of the crime charged against him, and she grew resolute under this conviction.

Her legal friend, the hero of this volume, spared no time nor pains to investigate the case, and he became satisfied that a conspiracy existed to prove young Armstrong a murderer, when another hand struck the fatal blow. This conviction induced him to undertake his defence with all the energy and ability he could bring to the task. But the public mind was intensely excited, and nearly every person was persuaded that the accused was guilty.

In these circumstances, it was more difficult to conduct the case, and Lincoln saw it in this light. He knew that it would be almost impossible to select an impartial jury at such a time, and he said to Mrs. Armstrong, "We must have the case put off if possible, until the excitement dies away."

"And let my dear boy lie in prison all the while?" she inquired.

"There is no other alternative. Better that than to be condemned and executed in advance."

"True, very true; but I am almost impatient to see him free again."

"That is not strange at all; but I am satisfied

that the case cannot be conducted impartially, while the public mind is so excited."

"I understand your views," said Mrs. Armstrong, "and shall agree to any decision you make. The case is in your hands, and you will conduct it as you think best."

"Another thing, too," added Mr. Lincoln; "I need more time to unravel this conspiracy. I believe that too much time cannot be spent in looking into the matter. I want to produce evidence that shall vindicate your son to the satisfaction of every reasonable man, and expose his accuser."

"You cannot desire it more than I do; and I think your views of the case are wise."

It was thus settled that the lawyer should secure a postponement of the case, if possible, and every exertion be made to unravel the affair. In this he was successful, and the case was deferred, much to the annoyance of many, who had made up their minds that the young man was guilty, and ought to be tried at once, and condemned.

The interim was spent in tracing evidence, and Mrs. Armstrong's counsellor labored as assiduously to pay his old debt of gratitude as he would have done under the offer of a fee of five thousand dollars.

We hasten to the trial. The time for it arrived, and it drew together a crowd of interested people. Nor were they under so much excitement as when the case was postponed. The "sober, second thought" had moderated their feelings, and they were in a better frame of mind to judge impartially.

The witnesses for the State were introduced; some to testify of Armstrong's previous vicious character, and others to relate what they saw of the affair on the night of the murder. His accuser testified in the most positive manner, that he saw him make the dreadful thrust that felled his victim.

"Could there be no mistake in regard to the person who struck the blow?" asked the counsel for the defence.

"None at all: I am confident of that," replied the witness.

"What time in the evening was it?"

"Between nine and ten o'clock."

"Well, about how far between? Was it quarter past nine or half past nine o'clock, or still later? Be more exact, if you please."

"I should think it might have been about half past nine o'clock," answered the witness.

"And you are confident that you saw the prisoner at the bar give the blow? Be particular in your testimony, and remember that you are under oath."

"I am; there can be no mistake about it."

"Was it not dark?"

"Yes; but the moon was shining brightly."

"Then it was not very dark, as there was a moon?"

"No; the moon made it light enough for me to see the whole affair."

"Be particular on this point. Do I understand you to say that the murder was committed about half past nine o'clock, and that the moon was shining brightly at the time?"

"Yes, that is what I testify."

"Very well; that is all."

His principal accuser was thus positive in his testimony, and the sagacious attorney saw enough therein to brand him as a perjurer.

After the witnesses for the State had been called, the defence introduced a few, to show that young Armstrong had borne a much better character than some of the witnesses gave him, and also that his accuser had been his personal enemy, while the murdered young man was his personal friend.

The counsel for the Commonwealth considered that the evidence was too strong against Armstrong to admit of a reasonable doubt of his guilt; therefore, his plea was short and formal.

All eyes were now turned to Lincoln. What could he say for the accused, in the face of such testimony? Few saw any possible chance for the supposed culprit to escape: his condemnation was sure.

Mr. Lincoln rose, while a deeply impressive stillness reigned throughout the court-room. The prisoner sat with a worried, despairing look, such as he had worn ever since his arrest. When he was led into the court-room, a most melancholy expression sat upon his brow, as if he were for saken by every friend, and the evidence presented was not suited to produce a change for the better.

His counsel proceeded to review the testimony, and called attention particularly to the discrepancies in the statements of the principal witness. What had seemed to the multitude as plain, truthful statements he showed to be wholly inconsistent with other parts of the testimony, indicating a plot against an innocent man. Then, raising his clear, full voice to a higher key, and lifting his long, wiry right arm above his head, as if about to annihilate his client's accuser, he exclaimed: "And he testifies that the moon was shining brightly when the deed was perpetrated, between the hours of nine and ten o'clock, when the moon did not appear on that night, as your Honor's almanac will show, until an hour or more later, and consequently the whole story is a fabrication."

The audience were carried by this sudden exposure of the accuser's falsehoods, and they were now as bitter against the principal witness as they were before against the supposed culprit.

Mr. Lincoln went on in a strain of singular enthusiasm and eloquence, portraying the deep, black guilt of the perjurer, and at the same time pointing his nervous finger at the false witness, and flashing his keen eye upon him, until he winced and writhed under the faithful scourge. The speaker appealed to the jury in behalf of their own sons, who might fall victims to the malice and revenge of some base wretch, and he besought them to remember the fatherless and the widow in the day of trial, referring to his own experience under the friendly roof of her whose son was arraigned before them, and the debt of gratitude which he was trying to liquidate; and eyes unused to weep were wet when he closed his fervid plea. It was near night when he concluded by saying, that, "If justice is done, as I believe it will be, before the sun sets, it will shine upon my client a free man."

Before he closed his plea, the wicked accuser was so overcome by the speaker's description of the perjurer's guilt, that he could not retain his seat, and he rose up, tremblingly, and fairly staggered out of the court-room.

"A vile perjurer!" whispered one spectator to another.

"That 's plain enough to see!" was the response.

"He carries his guilt in his face," said a third; "Armstrong is an innocent man."

"No doubt about that, and his accuser deserves the halter. It is bad as murder itself to undertake to prove an innocent man guilty of such a crime."

"Lucky for him that he did n't play the game with me," added the last speaker but one.

And so the feeling went round the court-room. They who had come thither with the full belief that Armstrong was the murderer, were now convinced of his innocence.

The jury retired, and the court adjourned for the day. But while the judge and counsellors were taking tea at the hotel, it was announced that the jury had returned. They had been out less than thirty minutes. At once there was a rush to the court-room, and it was filled to overflowing with a deeply-interested assembly.

As the prisoner came in, his mother leaning upon his arm, a gleam of hope could be discovered lighting up his brow a little, while his aged mother appeared less sad and broken-hearted. Amid an oppressive silence, when the beating of anxious hearts could almost be heard, the jury returned a verdict of "Not Guilty!"

A shout of joy rang through the court-room, and the mother sprang forward and fell into the arms of her guiltless son, who lifted her up, saying: "Mother, look upon your son again as free and innocent," and his utterance was choked, as he gazed into the pallid face of her who loved him as her own life.

"Thank God!" she exclaimed, rallying from her partial faintness, into which she had been thrown by excess of joy.

"Where is Mr. Lincoln?" inquired the acquit-

"It is not yet sundown, and you are free." — Page 303.

ted son, as the crowd pressed around him. Then seeing his tall form on the other side of the room, he pushed through the assembly, and grasped his deliverer by the hand; but he could not speak. His heart was too full for utterance. Tears filled his eyes, — tears of overflowing gratitude, — and he stood speechless before him, expressing more by his looks than he possibly could have done by words.

Turning his eye toward the setting sun, and still grasping the hand of his client, Mr. Lincoln said, "It is not yet sundown, and you are free."

The scene was too affecting to be witnessed with unmoistened eyes, and many observers turned away to conceal their emotion.

A rare incident this, illustrating both the noble character of Abraham Lincoln, and the precious truth that is contained in the promise, "Cast thy bread upon the waters, for thou shalt find it after many days."

Here and there we meet with similar incidents, although they are far between, and each one is a bright spot on the dark background of human nature. We love to recall and ponder them. One of this kind is recorded of an American statesman, who might have found an honored place in the history of our land, but for his treasonable acts. We refer to Hon. Alexander H. Stephens. With all his talents and promise of high renown, the part he has played in the wicked game of secession has consigned his name to undying shame. Notwithstanding this, however, the following fact of his early life, related by himself several years ago, at Alexandria, in an address in behalf of the orphan asylum and free schools of the city, will be read with interest: —

"A poor little boy, on a cold night in January, with no home or roof to shelter his head, no paternal or maternal guardian or guide to protect him on his way, reached at nightfall the house of a rich planter, who took him in, fed, lodged, and sent him on his way with his blessing. These kind attentions cheered his heart, and inspired him with fresh courage to battle with the obstacles of life. Years rolled round; Providence led him on; he had reached the legal profession; his host had died; the cormorants that prey on the substance of man had formed a conspiracy to get from the widow her estates. She sent for the nearest counsel, to commit her cause to him, and that counsel proved to be the orphan boy years before welcomed and entertained by her deceased husband. The stimulus of a warm and tenacious gratitude was now added to the ordinary motives connected with the profession. He undertook her cause with a will not easily to be resisted; he gained it; the widow's estates were secured to her in perpetuity; and, Mr. Stephens added, with an emphasis of emotion that sent its electric thrill through the house, 'That orphan boy stands before you!'"

Would that the promise of such a touching fact still cheered the life of this recreant son of Georgia! But alas! he arose as a star of the first magnitude, and then plunged, like a falling meteor, into the dark abyss of treason. How unlike the noble, patriotic efforts of the subject of this volume, who clings to the Union with the tenacity of one who is resolved to save it or perish!

XXVI.

CONCLUSION

WE have now traced the early life of the subject of this volume to the period when he began to win laurels in his chosen profession. We have seen him enter upon the stern duties of manhood with an empty pocket, but a noble heart. The pioneer boy has become the gifted lawyer.

His life, since the period at which our narrative stops, is known to all. His remarkable success in the legal profession, his efficiency in public offices, his connection with Congress, his position as President of the United States, and, what is better still, his untarnished character, have given him a world-wide fame.

That the foundation of his success was laid in his boyhood cannot be denied. We have seen that his early life was distinguished for those elements of character that have rendered his manhood conspicuous. An excellent mother's training appears in the beginning. Never was maternal influence more clearly illustrated in the rearing of a son. The three lessons that the mother of Washington said she endeavored to impress upon the mind of her son — namely, "obedience, diligence, and truth" — were insisted upon in his childhood. Never did a boy give more earnest heed to these cardinal virtues than did he. All along through his early life they appear, — the flower and fruit of a sainted mother's fidelity.

There was also an energy, perseverance, and decision manifest in all his acts, that augur well for the possessor. These qualities appear even in the sports of his boyhood. They characterize his early labors and studies.

Nor was the habit of doing things well absent in his case. Whether it was work, study, or play, everything was thoroughly done. And this quality served him better than teachers or money. Judge Douglas, his political antagonist, said of him, in a speech in 1858, "Lincoln is one of those peculiar men who perform with admirable skill everything they undertake." It was just as true of him at twelve years of age as it was at fifty.

Then his studious habits and love of books made him thoughtful, discriminating, and stable. In this way his mental powers were developed with his physical. The mind and the body strengthened together. Small advantages produced great results.

Self-control was an important characteristic of his early life. He did not use profane language when other boys did. He would forego the pleasures of companionship to assist his parents. He could sacrifice a good time in frolic for the enjoyment of reading a book. Though living when almost every one used intoxicating drinks, he kept his appetite in subjection, and practised remarkable abstinence. Says one who was a companion with him from ten to twenty-two years of age, "He was remarkably temperate. In all the gatherings where they used intoxicating liquors (and they were many) I never saw him take the smallest dram."

He never felt above his business. He was never ashamed of his origin or his poverty. When consulted with regard to the incidents of his early life, he remarked: "You can find the whole of my early life in a single line of Gray's Elegy, —

'The short and simple annals of the poor.'"

With this noble spirit, from youth to age, he has pursued the even tenor of his way, thereby honoring himself, and adding dignity to the offices he has filled.

There is no doubt that the connection of his ancestors with the hardships and struggles of the fathers for existence and independence, made known to him in the thrilling tales of border wars, and Revolutionary battles, served to develop that courage, patriotism, and deep interest in his country's welfare for which he has been justly honored.

We can trace a connection, also, between his

early instructions and experience on the subject of slavery, and that honest and consistent opposition to the cruel system, for which his later life has been distinguished. He has ever been a fearless defender of the rights of humanity.

The small library that he enjoyed in his early years was exactly suited to make him the man that he is. The Bible, Pilgrim's Progress, Æsop's Fables, Life of Washington, Life of Franklin, Life of Clay, and Plutarch's Lives, — what books more suitable to be read by a youth, who is destined to act a conspicuous part in the history of his country!

The labors and hardships of his early life, too, were just adapted to develop his physical nature into remarkable powers of endurance, as if a wise Providence was preparing him for the responsibilities of the present hour, under which ordinary constitutions would fail.

But, more than all, his unquestioned HONESTY reaches back from the present to his artless childhood. The fruit of maternal guidance, it adorned his boyhood and youth, as it has his manhood and age. It has given him an enviable fame. To this he owes the confidence that is reposed in his character. To this he is really indebted for his election to the Presidency of the United States. It aided him, at least, very materially, in working his way from the log-cabin to the White House. The times, the country, our destiny, demanded "an honest man, — the noblest work of God." And such was the Pioneer Boy of the West, whose unblemished youth foreshadowed the strict integrity of his manhood. In this connection, we may add, that a person who has enjoyed unusual facilities for judging, as his friend and neighbor for many years, writes as follows: "I have known him long and well, and I can say, in truth, I think (take him altogether) he is the best man I ever saw. Although he has never made a public profession of religion, I nevertheless believe that he has the fear of God before his eyes, and that he goes daily to a throne of grace, and asks wisdom, light, and knowledge, to enable him faithfully to discharge his duties."

The young reader, then, cannot fail to observe the connection between his early and later life. The man is what the boy was. As he sowed, so he reaps. His success is not mere luck, — it is the achievement of certain qualities of mind and heart. And in this regard, his life is a bright example for the youth of our beloved land to imitate. View it, reader, — study it, — copy it, — remembering that, like him, you must be the "artificer of your own fortune," — and you will not live in vain.

THE END.

Cambridge: Stereotyped and Printed by Welch, Bigelow, & Co.

THE FARMER BOY PLAYING SOLDIER.

www.ingramcontent.com/pod-product-compliance
Lightning Source LLC
LaVergne TN
LVHW020226110826
845151LV00003B/840

* 9 7 8 1 4 2 5 5 3 1 7 2 0 *